A few moments later, Dyson returned with a gurney, upon which lay a white-sheet–covered corpse. *Maybe this wasn't such a good idea,* Jenna thought.

When he pulled the sheet off, grinning at Jenna, he looked like a magician particularly proud of his latest trick. Her stomach churned as she stared at the dead man, whose body was bloated and pale, except in the dark areas under the skin on the backs of his legs and on his back, as if that entire side of his body were one huge blood blister.

Dr. Slikowski turned on a tape recorder that hung above the table.

"Subject, Nicholas Garson; autopsy 433-958-01," he began. "Caucasian male. Age thirty-four. Height, five feet ten inches; weight, one hundred ninety-seven pounds. Contusions reflecting struggle with hospital orderlies. Abdominal scar from apparent appendix removal. . . ."

He reached out and Dyson handed him a scalpel. *Here we go,* Jenna thought, swallowing hard. Jenna tried not to let her expression show what she was feeling inside, but her stomach was a bit queasy, and she shivered as the blade glided through flesh.

Just when Jenna thought Dr. Slikowski had forgotten all about their interview, he glanced up at her.

"So, Miss Blake, tell me about yourself."

Body of Evidence thrillers
by Christopher Golden

Body Bags
Thief of Hearts
(coming soon)

Available from Pocket Books

christopher golden

BODY BAGS

A *Body of Evidence*
thriller starring Jenna Blake

AN ARCHWAY PAPERBACK
Published by POCKET BOOKS
New York London Toronto Sydney Tokyo Singapore

AN ARCHWAY PAPERBACK *Original*

An Archway Paperback published by
POCKET BOOKS, a division of Simon & Schuster Inc.
1230 Avenue of the Americas, New York, NY 10020

ISBN: 0-671-03492-8

First Archway Paperback printing May 1999

10 9 8 7 6 5 4 3 2 1

AN ARCHWAY PAPERBACK and colophon are registered
trademarks of Simon & Schuster Inc.

Front cover illustration by Kamil Vojnar

Printed in the U.S.A.

for Jennifer Keates

acknowledgments

Thanks, as always, to Connie and the boys; Lucy Russo; my agent, Lori Perkins; my much-worshipped editor, Lisa Clancy, and her assistant, Elizabeth Shiflett; and my regular crew, José Nieto, Tom Sniegoski, Nancy Holder, Jeff Mariotte, Bob Tomko, and Stefan Nathanson.

Very special thanks, this time out, to my mother, Roberta Golden, and to Dr. Dean Pappas, Dr. Brian Golden, Dr. Cheryl Hanau, and Jennifer Keates.

A note of fondness, in closing, to everyone I spent time with "on the hill."

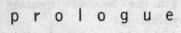

prologue

Amanda Green died for a cigarette.

Wednesday morning at 10:30, she rode the elevator down to the first floor of the courthouse, stepped off, and started toward the row of metal detectors and security guards that blocked her view of the doors. She'd been trying to quit smoking, and had winnowed her habit down to six cigarettes a day, each one of them on a rigid schedule. Once upon a time, half past ten had been her coffee break. Now it was time for a smoke.

She paused as she neared the security checkpoint. A cigarette already dangled from her mouth—she had taken it out while still on the elevator—but now she was searching around in her purse for her lighter, growing more and more frustrated because she couldn't find it.

Loud voices drew her attention. Amanda glanced up to see a neatly dressed young guy—a very good-

1

looking young guy—snapping at the security guard, who was waving a curling-iron–sized metal detector over him.

"Do the words 'I'm late' have any meaning to you?" the young guy shouted.

Amanda caught a look at his eyes and decided that he wasn't just angry, he was a little . . . off. But that was the security guard's business, not hers.

"Mr. Garson," the guard replied, "you'll have to keep your voice down, or you'll be denied entrance into the courthouse."

The young guy in the nice suit—Mr. Garson, apparently—snorted loudly. As they waved him through, he said something about Congressman Poulos being less than pleased. Amanda smiled at that. Valerie Poulos was about to go on trial upstairs on driving-under-the-influence charges. *This must be the lawyer the girl's congressman father hired,* she thought.

And that was all she thought. More pressing matters concerned her now. For she could not find that lighter, no matter how many times she rifled through her purse. The clock was ticking away her "coffee" break, and she was without a lighter. There were plenty of people around who she could ask for a book of matches, but so few people actually smoked these days that it wasn't as simple as it had once been.

With a sigh of frustration, Amanda moved toward a marble column just inside the row of metal detectors and crouched down. She set her purse down on the floor and began a more methodical search. The cigarette still dangled from her lips. At last, her fingers brushed the cold silver casing of her lighter, and Amanda smiled.

"Thank you, God," she whispered as she pulled the lighter out.

She stood, slinging her purse over her shoulder, the lighter clutched in her left hand. The sound of strident footsteps approaching made her turn, and she looked up just in time to see Mr. Garson bearing down on her. His eyes were wide with fury, his lip curled back in disgust, and a bit of drool slid down his chin.

Amanda had a moment to be disgusted and a little afraid before Nick Garson whipped his hard brown leather briefcase around and slammed her in the side of the face with it.

The cigarette flew from her mouth and skittered across the floor.

She let out a shriek and began cursing loudly at the man, even as she turned back to face him again. But Garson was already reaching for her. He grabbed a handful of her hair, hauled her up with one hand, his strength astonishing, and screamed in her face, foamy spittle flying from his lips.

"*No smoking!*" he roared.

Garson grabbed the back of her dress, bunching the fabric, with his free hand, and using her hair to guide her, he slammed her headfirst into the marble column. Her skull cracked.

Then he did it again.

When Garson let Amanda's body fall to the floor, there was a wide streak of blood on the column.

The nearest security guard was William Campagna.

He was only a few feet away when Garson killed Amanda Green, and Campagna was a bit shell-shocked. Not to mention enraged by the madman's actions. Shouting furiously, Willy Campagna reached for Garson's right hand—the hand that held the briefcase—and pulled it behind the man's back. The briefcase fell to the floor and Campagna kicked it away. He shoved Garson's arm up nearly hard enough to break it, propelling him toward the wall, getting ready to handcuff the lunatic and put him into custody.

Willy Campagna had been taught that hold at the academy. There was no way to get out of it without breaking your arm.

With a scream of rage and pain, Nick Garson spun out of Campagna's hold. He didn't even flinch when his arm broke in two different places. By then he'd moved in close to Campagna and used his good left hand to snatch the guard's pistol from its holster.

He was foaming at the mouth like a rabid dog as he shot Willy Campagna through the heart.

Several other guards were coming toward him then, weapons drawn. When they saw Campagna go down, they all stopped, raised their weapons, and began to shout warnings at Garson.

Garson fired three times—killing Tricia Carlisle and wounding Seth Blum—before a bullet from Blum's service weapon struck him in the shoulder and spun him around. The gun flew from Garson's hand. His red, wild eyes darted about, taking in the blood-spattered marble lobby.

Then he began to scream. He fell to his knees,

curled up in a ball on the floor, weeping uncontrolla-
bly and shuddering as if he were about to go into
convulsions. His shattered arm jutted out at an odd
angle from his shoulder.

As the surviving guards moved in, Garson stopped
moving abruptly and fell silent.

Blood was leaking from his ears.

"Oh, man," muttered one of the guards, poking at
Garson with his right foot. "Somebody call for an
ambulance."

Blum glanced around the lobby and shook his head
in horror. "Better make that two," he said, and then
slumped to the floor, weak from loss of blood.

"And tell them to bring some body bags."

chapter 1

It was a beautiful day to grow up.

There had been a storm the day before, a heavy, drenching rain. But that morning the sun was out, the sky was blue and perfect, and everything just seemed to sparkle.

Or, thought Jenna Blake, as she steered her mother's Volvo wagon along Route 16, *maybe it's just me*.

The frantic city life of Boston was only a few miles distant from Somerset, Massachusetts, but with the light breeze blowing through the trees, it might have been an entire world away. The Volvo's radio blasted tunes from her mother's misspent youth in the seventies, and Jenna sang happily along. She loved her mom. But she figured she'd love her even more after today.

What was that old saying? Oh, yeah, "Absence makes the heart grow fonder."

Jenna was going to be loving her mother to death in a few hours.

It was her first day at college.

"Watch out!" her mother snapped.

Jenna swerved slightly to go around the banged-up Toyota that had stopped suddenly just ahead of them, intent upon a left turn the driver hadn't bothered to signal for. With a sigh, Jenna raised her eyebrows and glanced over at her mom.

"I know how to drive, Mom," she said.

Dr. April Blake relaxed into an easy smile. "So do all the other people who have accidents. Please pay attention to the road."

"I'm all about attention," Jenna declared. Then she glanced over at her mother.

The two of them had been chatting happily throughout the forty-minute drive from home—in Natick, Massachusetts—to Somerset, just north of Cambridge and Boston, within spitting distance of Harvard and M.I.T. Somerset was a college town, no doubt, and Somerset University, Somerset Medical School, and Somerset Medical Center sprawled over many acres of prime real estate. It had been one of the most respected universities in the nation since its founding more than a century and a half earlier, even if—as her mother had mentioned more than once—it wasn't Ivy League.

Her mom had wanted her to go to Harvard.

Fortunately, that hatchet had been buried months earlier, so the Harvard issue didn't come up at all on the drive east. In fact, her mom seemed pretty happy about the whole deal, and they'd laughed and gossiped the whole trip. They'd talked about the school. They'd talked about the campus and about friends of Jenna's who had already left or would soon go off to begin their own new lives at colleges and universities all over the country.

Moira Kearney had been Jenna's best friend since the first grade. Freshman year in high school, they'd met Priya Lahiri for the first time, and from then on, the three were inseparable. All for one and one for all. Until Priya started dating Noah Levine, who just happened to be Moira's ex, and it got ugly from there. Senior year, nothing had been the same. Now they'd all moved on—Moira to USC, Priya to Northwestern, and Noah to Umass Amherst. Jenna was sad at the separation, no question. But things had been so strange that she wondered if communicating via e-mail and seeing one another at Thanksgiving and Christmas and over the summer might not be all they could handle. It was especially difficult for Jenna, because she'd remained close to all three of them.

"This will be really good for you," her mother said, after they'd hashed out the weirdnesses of her friends one more time. "New faces, new ideas. Trust me."

"Always," Jenna replied.

They talked about the latest e-mail Jenna had received from Yoshiko Kitsuta, who was going to be Jenna's roommate for freshman year. Jenna was excited about meeting Yoshiko in person at last, but also a bit weirded out about having to share a room with someone for the first time. She had a much older half brother, but they'd never even lived in the same house together, and Jenna knew her mother had spoiled her.

They talked about Jenna's dad, who'd be meeting them for lunch after they'd moved her things into the dorm. They talked about a lot of things—everything—except the one thing they were both avoiding. What they hadn't talked about, not directly at least, was the fact that when April drove away from Somerset that day, she'd be leaving her only child behind. Jenna knew it had to be bothering her mom.

Now, after a brief pause in their conversation, Jenna looked straight ahead, obediently watching the road, and asked, "How're you holding up, Mom?"

"I'm fine, honey," her mother said. "You're not *that* bad a driver."

Jenna glanced over at her quickly. "That's not what I meant."

April reached out a hand and brushed her daughter's dark hair out of her eyes.

"I know what you meant, Jenna," she said. "I'll be fine. I'm going to miss you. The house won't be nearly as chaotic and the phone won't be ringing off the hook and I'll have to drive an hour to do mother-daughter self-indulgence shopping days, but I'll be all right.

"I'm very proud of you."

Jenna grinned. "Thanks, Mom. You're not so bad yourself, for an old lady." She paused for a long moment, and then slowly said, "I . . ."

"Don't bother," April interrupted, waving her hand in the air. "Don't even try to pretend you aren't completely psyched to be here, that you aren't champing at the bit to have your own life, make your own decisions."

"Mom!" Jenna said, eyes wide. "You know I'm . . ."

"Yes, you'll miss me," April laughed. "I know. But you've always wanted to grow up too fast, Jenna. In junior high, you couldn't wait for high school. In high school, you couldn't wait for college."

Jenna's mother glanced out the window as they drove into the small downtown area of Somerset. Even here, there were beautiful trees beyond the buildings and in small parks and public areas they passed. As she glanced at her mother again, Jenna couldn't think of a single thing to say.

Her mom was right.

"Do me a favor, though, sweetheart," April added, turning to look at Jenna again. "Don't be in a rush to get out of here, okay? Enjoy it. You'll never have more time, or more freedom, just to be Jenna, than you will in the next four years. Savor it."

"I will, Mom. I promise," Jenna replied. "And I'll call and keep you in the loop, and ask for advice about boys, and all that."

April shook her head and chuckled. "No, you won't," she said. "Oh, I'm sure we'll talk all the time. But you'll have friends here for all the really important girl talks. If you're planning to run off and get married, though, let me know, all right?"

"Mom!" Jenna said, scandalized. "Please!"

But in spite of her playful response, Jenna was bothered by something her mother had said. The thing about friends. She was nervous about that. Classes,

11

she could take. Teachers, she could handle. Living on her own was a dream come true. But making new friends . . . she was terrified by the thought of it.

As if college doesn't have enough pressure without the whole "fitting-in" issue, she thought. *I might as well introduce myself as outcast and social misfit, and have it done with.*

As though she could read her daughter's mind, April patted her hand. "Don't worry, Jenna. It's going to be great."

Jenna was about to respond, to tell her mother about her other major fear, when the homes and delis and mom-and-pop shops on the right-hand side disappeared and the ground suddenly rose up into a tree-covered hill. At the peak of the hill, over the tops of trees and several buildings, she could see the spire of Brunswick Chapel and two of the larger dormitories.

As she guided the car along, they passed several of the academic buildings, which were nearer to the street. There was a fence between the road and the university grounds, and a little ways on, it lifted up into an enormous wrought-iron archway. Jenna slowed the car—several drivers beeped angrily as they passed her on the left—and she stared past her mother through the arch and up Memorial Steps, a set of granite and marble stairs that led up the hill to the main campus.

"Wow," she said.

"You've been here before," her mother reminded her.

"Yeah," Jenna agreed. "But now it's *mine.*"

April laughed at that, and they drove on. A short way up, they turned right on Sterling Lane and drove into the heart of the campus. Past dormitories, the library, and the campus center, and several homes that had been converted into student or faculty housing, or university offices. Jenna knew from her tour of the school that Coleman Auditorium, where most of Somerset's theatrical productions were staged, was one street over. One of these days she might actually get up the guts to appear on that stage.

Jenna took another right, onto Fletcher Avenue, and they were driving up the hill past the home of the university president. Then they were at the top of the hill, directly in front of Sparrow Hall, the building that would be Jenna's home for the next year. The outside was all stone and mortar, with gothic peaks and ledges.

"It really is a beautiful campus," her mother said.

Jenna looked out her mother's window again, and saw the main academic quad. It was a broad stretch of the campus that was nothing but a perfectly green lawn, dotted by enormous, ancient shade trees and lined on either side by academic buildings and the chapel. There were paved paths weaving in and out of the quad, but no roads. No cars allowed. It was a place not for coming and going, but for learning.

"I think I'm going to like it here," Jenna announced.

Her mother laughed. "Well, that's a relief. You took long enough to decide."

"Hey, since when did you get to be sarcasto-chick?"

Jenna chided her. "I thought that was my job as resident teenager."

"It was. But you're not resident teenager anymore. You have to be a grown-up now, which means I don't."

Jenna smiled and shook her head.

"It's going to be great," April said. "I just know it. And you'll be able to spend a lot more time with your father."

Jenna bit her lip. That was her other great fear, besides making friends. Her parents had been divorced for twelve years. Her father, Dr. Frank Logan, taught at Somerset. Up until now, she'd seen him twice a year, at best. She didn't know what to expect from her father, now that she was going to be seeing him all the time.

"You guys aren't gonna be fighting over me, are you?" Jenna asked.

"Fighting?" April asked. "Probably. Over you? No."

They stared out at Sparrow Hall and at the quad for a few more seconds, and then Jenna said, "Well, I guess we'd better unpack."

Lugging suitcases, a trunk, a television set, a VCR, boxes of computer equipment, and milk crates filled with books and compact discs up three flights of stairs turned out to be a decent way to meet at least a few people. Jenna was a bit disappointed that Yoshiko hadn't arrived yet, but they had all year to get to know one another, she reasoned. April got to talking with several other parents who were also moving their kids in, and Jenna met a handful of other freshmen, most of whose names she forgot the moment she met the next one.

Well, there was a cute guy named Erik. She remembered *his* name.

She also wished she had worn something else. Jeans and a tank top were good clothes to move boxes around in, but not so good when it came to making a first impression. Still, everybody seemed friendly, and she was relieved to find out that most of the upperclassmen hadn't returned to the dorms yet. The next day, Friday, was orientation, but classes didn't actually begin until Monday.

Jenna and her mother also met Aaron and Debbie Felber, the resident directors of Sparrow Hall. They lived in the building and were, essentially, the dorm managers. The Felbers were fortyish, both a little gray, and a bit odd. Kind of distant. On the other hand, Jenna figured they had seen dozens of freshmen trooping through the door this morning. It had to be a little overwhelming.

Sparrow 311. That was her dorm room. It was in a long tiled hallway with a large carpeted common area right in the middle for students to hang out or study. The girls were on one end, the guys on the other. Number 311 was about halfway between the common area and the girls' bathroom, which also had a row of showers.

"I'm not sure I like you being this close to so many boys," April said, after their third trip up the stairs.

"I'll let you know how it goes," Jenna replied, as she lugged a heavy box filled with shoes down the hall to her room.

She loved her room.

It wasn't much, actually. There were two enormous windows—big enough to sit in and play the guitar on a warm day; if she'd taken guitar lessons instead of learning to play piano—as well as a pair of closets, a pair of bureaus, a pair of desks, and a sink with a mirror above it. The beds were bunked, but it was clear they didn't have to be. She figured she'd ask Yoshiko what her preference was.

In her mind's eye, she decorated the room even before they'd brought all of her things up. It would be hard to hang posters, or anything else for that matter, on the cinderblock wall, but she'd figure something out. Planks and milk crates would make passable bookshelves and an entertainment unit. While Jenna had brought the TV and VCR, Yoshiko was bringing her stereo and a little fridge that they both knew they couldn't live without.

Of course, their computers would go on their desks, leaving little space for actually doing anything by hand on top of them. But, hey, nothing was more important than being jacked in, and the dorms were wired to the Internet. Jenna thought she'd actually have a much easier time staying close to her high school friends than her mom had had, because she could e-mail them all whenever she wanted. No huge long-distance bills. That was a plus.

After the fourth trip, Jenna put her hands on her hips, glanced at her mother, and frowned.

"What?" April asked.

"We need some things, here. Coffeemaker. Hot plate. Toaster oven."

"Is that even allowed?" her mother asked.

Jenna raised an eyebrow at that. She'd have to check the student handbook.

When they were done carrying the boxes, she had a few minutes to herself while her mother went to move the car to somewhere where it wouldn't get towed. They still had three-quarters of an hour before they had to meet her father for lunch. She looked around at the boxes, thought about starting to put her clothes away, then decided to procrastinate for a few more minutes.

She bounced on the lower bunk, found the bed quite uncomfortable, realized there was nothing she could do about it, and shrugged. Jenna got up and walked to the window, really checking out her view for the first time.

And what a view it is. Sparrow was at the top of the hill, so even though she was only on the third floor, she had a good view of a couple of other dorms, and then, beyond them, of the town of Somerset, stretching out toward Cambridge, and Boston beyond. From the roof of Mayer Library, she recalled from her tour, one could actually see the Boston skyline.

"I'm back," her mother said, entering through the open door.

Jenna jumped, then laughed at herself.

17

After Jenna hooked up her computer, a priority even though she wouldn't have e-mail until phone service was turned on, they set about putting away some of her clothes. Jenna and her mother arranged them in the closet she chose—Yoshiko's bad luck for not arriving first—and then stowed the rest in the drawers of her single dresser. They were both amazed that she managed to fit everything.

"The entertainment center will have to wait until we buy the wood," her mother said, glancing at her watch. "We're going to be late."

They weren't late, actually. Or, rather, they were early in comparison to Jenna's father, who showed up twenty minutes after they'd arrived at DePasquale Brothers, an Italian restaurant a mile from campus. He'd said the faculty frequented the restaurant, but Jenna didn't think anybody actually "frequented" the place, by the look of it. It was a ghost town, but they were definitely open for business. One thing she was sure of, students didn't hang here.

She'd have to find out where the off-campus hangouts actually were. As soon as she had the chance.

The hostess gave them a table by the window, and Jenna sat watching for her dad. She hadn't seen him for nearly two months, and she was looking forward to it, despite her anxiety about getting to know him better.

Before leaving her dorm, Jenna had taken the time to change into black jeans and new sneakers, both of which she'd bought the day before, and a bone-white ribbed cotton T-shirt she'd gotten over the summer at Abercrombie.

She wanted to look nice for her dad, but not too nice. If she dressed up, she'd only be uncomfortable. Her mom always looked good. She was a doctor, a surgeon, actually, and even in surgery, under her scrubs, she had class. Dr. April Blake made it all look so easy. It was something Jenna aspired to, but didn't think she'd ever achieve.

Looking at her mother now, she thought her first step in that direction would be a pair of those imitation suede leggings in that weird coppery color. They went well with her hair, which, like Jenna's, was a dark auburn.

"There he is," April said.

Jenna looked out the window and saw her father striding across the street in front of the restaurant.

Frank Logan was a shade over six feet tall, and had a beard that was equal parts brown and gray. His dark hair had a little while to go before it was as gray as the beard, but it wouldn't be long. He wore a nice tie over a white shirt, and tan pants with brown loafers. The clothes were fine, but somehow they just didn't hang right on her father. Nothing seemed to. The tie was a bit loose, the shirt badly tucked in, the pants riding a little too low.

He was rumpled, as always. But as she watched him approach the door, Jenna felt a surge of love for her father.

Maybe it would be nice, getting to know him, she thought. *Spending more time with him.* As long as he knew that, after all these years, it wasn't time for him to start "parenting" her. Jenna was eighteen years old, and she wanted to make sure that her father didn't forget that.

"Hey!" Frank said happily as he walked toward their table.

Jenna smiled as she went to hug him. Her father embraced her tightly.

"Hi, Daddy," she mumbled into his shoulder as he hugged her.

"I'm so glad you're here, sweetheart," he said. "This is going to be quite a year, I think. How's your dorm?"

"Totally rocks," Jenna said happily.

Then she turned to her mother, who was also standing, across the small table. Her father released her and looked over at his ex-wife with a smile, but Jenna felt the distance between them. She hated it. Always had. But life was like that sometimes.

"Hello, April," her father said.

"Frank," her mother replied.

With a soft chuckle, her dad moved around the table and kissed her mom on the cheek.

"Why don't we order?" he suggested. "I'm absolutely starved. The gnocchi is really something here, by the way."

They all sat down then, and in between answering her father's questions, and listening to the two of them discuss other matters, relating to tuition and financial aid—all of which seemed to be perfectly friendly conversation—Jenna decided that they might not actually have an argument after all.

Which would be a refreshing switch. There was a reason her parents usually only saw one another on Christmas.

Still, to her surprise, they'd actually gotten almost all the way through the meal before her dad brought up the subject of majors. Jenna saw her mother's eyes narrow at the mention of it. They'd had this conversation in the past.

"She's just a freshman, Frank," Jenna's mom chided. "She has plenty of time to worry about what she'll major in. Your daughter has a lot of interests."

Ouch! Jenna thought. It would have been impossible for her father to miss the real point of what her mom was saying: *your daughter has a lot of interests you don't know about because you weren't around to find out.*

Sometimes the truth hurt.

"I know that," her dad said, sighing. "It was just a question, April. College is all about exploring. I was just curious. Is that all right?"

The conversation went on that way for a while, and Jenna played with her spaghetti, picked at her chicken cutlet, but mainly just watched traffic go by or studied the cartoonish map of Italy on her place mat. She wanted to leave. Mainly because she knew where the conversation was headed.

Jenna didn't want to go there.

The moment the pitch of her mother's voice started to rise, she held up a hand.

"Hold it!" she snapped.

21

Her parents turned to stare at her.

"Jenna's life," she said. "Change the subject."

And they did. The rest of the meal was eaten amidst cordial discussions of politics and which movies they had all seen, and then, when it was all over, Jenna's mother stood up.

"Well," she said, "I guess it's time for me to go."

Jenna and her mother hugged for a long time. When they separated, she saw that there were tears starting to well up in her mom's eyes, and she felt a sudden burning in her own.

"Stop it," she said, laughing a bit. "You're going to make me cry."

"Call me as soon as your phone is turned on," April said.

"I'll call you tomorrow, but it might be collect," Jenna replied, wiping her eyes.

Then her mother did something that surprised Jenna. She turned and pulled Jenna's dad into a hug, the first sign of affection she'd seen them exchange in many years.

"Please take care of our little girl," April pleaded.

Frank grinned and kissed the top of his ex-wife's head. "Don't worry. I'll keep her out of trouble."

"Hey!" Jenna protested. "What if there's trouble I *want* to get into?"

Both her parents laughed at that. But Jenna was serious.

When her mother had gone, her father smiled and leaned across the table as if he were sharing a secret.

"So," he said, "really, have you thought about majors at all? There are a lot of ways to get a head start, depending on what you want to do."

Jenna narrowed her eyes. "I don't want to be a lawyer."

"I know!" her father said, throwing up his hands. "You've told me that a million times. And I don't blame you. Why do you think I teach criminology instead of practice it?"

Professor Frank Logan taught more than criminology, actually. The acutal titles of the classes he was instructing this semester were Intro to Criminal Psychology, The Fundamentals of Law, and Law and Society, among others. And Jenna couldn't deny that she found some of it truly fascinating. But she didn't want to be a cop, and she didn't want to be a lawyer.

"Your mother wants you to be a doctor, of course," Frank added.

"Of course," Jenna admitted.

"And?"

"And I might be okay with that. I mean, I love the idea of helping people, and there's something so vital about being a surgeon, something you provide to people that makes what lawyers provide seem really . . . I don't know . . ."

"Cheap?" her father offered.

"You said it, not me," Jenna agreed, with a shrug and a grin.

"So premed," Frank said, nodding.

"No pressure or anything, huh, Dad?" Jenna said, growing a bit annoyed.

"Your mother and I both want what's best for you, Jenna. You know that. I'd just like to see you have every possible advantage," he explained. "If you want to be a doctor . . ."

"I'll faint."

Her father looked at her, confused.

Jenna sighed. "When I see someone bleeding," she confessed, "I get nauseated and dizzy. I could never be a surgeon. I'll faint. Plus, the idea that I might screw up and accidentally kill someone terrifies me."

Frank raised his eyebrows, shook his head in slight amusement, and then ran the fingers of his right hand over his beard. Thinking. Stroking the beard, always a sign of deep thought from her dad. After a moment, his eyes seemed to light up.

"What?" Jenna asked.

"You'd like to be a doctor, but you can't stand to see someone bleed?" he asked.

"Right," she agreed.

"And you're worried that you could make a mistake and cause a patient's death?"

"Yeah. So?"

Frank tilted his head and smiled mischievously. "What if your patients were already dead?"

c h a p t e r 2

It was midafternoon by the time Professor Logan turned down Lewis Street and guided his beat-up Toyota into the driveway of the house he shared with two other professors. Jenna's father lived on the second floor. The first-floor resident was Shayna Emerson, an English literature professor whom Jenna had always hoped her father would get up the courage to ask on a date. Shayna was fortyish, and—to Jenna's mind—a bit too thin and a bit too pale. But she was cute and funny and very intelligent, and she seemed to like Jenna's father well enough.

The third floor was occupied by José Mattei, who was a professor of political science and international relations, and who happened to be one of her father's best friends. Professor Mattei had also been assigned as her faculty advisor, which Jenna thought was ultra-convenient. The two men denied it, but Jenna figured that Professors Logan and Mattei were neck deep in a conspiracy to keep an eye on her. *Let them,* she thought. *I'm a big girl now. Old enough to make my own mistakes.*

"Penny for your innermost secrets," her father said.

Jenna blinked. She'd been drifting, and with good reason. It had already been a wild day—maybe the most exciting day of her life, though very little had happened. *Except for that whole first day of college thing,* she thought, smiling to herself. But add to that her father's idea—a suggestion for her career track that had taken her totally by surprise.

I mean, a medical examiner? she thought.

"Dad," she said flatly. "Okay, gross? We're talking about dead people here."

"Well," said her father, reasonably, "it might solve your problem with bleeding, and, let's face it, when you're dealing with a corpse, you don't have to worry about making a fatal mistake."

She stared at him. "Dad, that's disgusting."

But she was thinking about it.

As they got out of the car, Jenna shivered. The perfect day had gotten a bit chilly for her. *Not so perfect after all,* she thought.

"You want a jacket?" her father asked as they trudged up to the door and he rattled his key ring around looking for the house key.

"I have one in my room. A lot more than one, actually," she replied with a small laugh. "Sorry. I'm totally disoriented. This whole college thing seems a little surreal still."

"Look around," her father said.

26

Jenna did. There were station wagons and U-Hauls and kids with boxes and crates and suitcases and home electronics . . . just about everywhere she looked.

"It's surreal to all of them, no matter what anybody tries to tell you," he said. "But in a week it'll be second nature to you. You won't be able to remember what it was like living with your mother."

Jenna raised an eyebrow and shot him a questioning glance.

"No, that wasn't a dig," he said, turning the key and pushing the door open. "Just a fact of life. I don't think you're going to have any trouble getting settled in here, Jenna."

She smiled. *Maybe it'll be nice hanging out with Dad,* she thought as she followed him into the house, and up the stairs to the left.

"Of course she won't," came a heavily accented voice.

At the top of the second-floor landing, Professor Mattei was carrying a slim briefcase and a stack of books, and trying desperately not to drop the awkward burden. Since she had last seen him, the professor had grown a thin goatee, and she thought it looked charming on him. He smiled down at Jenna, and she grinned broadly.

She'd only met the man three or four times, but he was very kind.

"Hello, Professor," she said.

"Jenna," the man said, and sighed, "please call me José. Except in class, of course."

As he passed them on the stairs, barely managing

to keep his books from falling, he looked at Jenna's dad. "She'll do fine, Frank. And even better than fine if you don't haunt her. In fact, as her advisor, I'm going to see that you don't stifle her growth."

"Hey!" Frank protested, wrapping an arm around Jenna and pulling her to him. "I want to spend time with my little girl. She's living right up the street, after all. But I'm not going to hang around all the time. She needs space, and we both have work to do."

Professor Mattei laughed, then looked at Jenna and winked. "He's only repeating what I told him last night," the man said, and chuckled.

They parted ways, and Jenna followed her dad to the door of his second-floor apartment. Inside, he put a pot on for tea, a habit he'd picked up from Shayna, downstairs, and they talked for a little while about which professors were the most popular among the students and which of the campus's half dozen dining halls attracted which cliques.

"You'll probably want to meet some of the theater kids," he said. "They usually hang out in Morrissey Dining Hall. That's also where most of the foreign students eat."

Jenna didn't have the heart to tell her father that she really wanted to find out about all those things on her own. So they sat and she asked questions, and he answered them, and before she knew it, it was almost four o'clock.

"Dad, this is great, just hanging out. But it's going to be dinnertime in a little while. I really should get back and see if my roomie has shown up. Maybe we can set up the rest of the room."

Frank started to get up from the sofa. "Do you need any help?" he asked. "Maybe I could . . ."

"I'm sure you have things to do," she said. "How about if you come by my dorm tomorrow and we'll go to lunch."

"All right, honey," her father said. "Sorry if I'm overdoing it. I guess I just feel like . . ." he paused, eyed her closely. "Like I've got a lot of overdoing it to do. You know what I mean?"

In reply, Jenna leaned over and kissed his head. "Yeah, Dad. And you're doing just fine. I'm in Sparrow 311. Can't wait for you to see the room."

She moved toward the door.

"Hey, Jenna?"

Halfway out the door, she turned and looked at him.

"You know, I'm sort of friendly with the medical examiner over at the teaching hospital; fellow named Walter Slikowski. They're always looking for assistants this time of year. If you're interested, I could give him a call. That way you could see if that sort of thing interested you at all."

Jenna blinked. She opened her mouth, about to make some wise remark about dead bodies again. But then she thought about it. There were a lot of things about the idea that appealed to her. She was interested in maybe being a doctor someday, with all the previously stated reservations, of course. Plus, a medical examiner was usually called upon to find the answers to questions that puzzled everyone else. Jenna liked that.

"You know what?" she said. "That would be great. Hey, what's the totally worst thing that could happen. I puke on him, right?"

Her father looked horrified, and Jenna laughed and shrugged.

"Good thing he's a friend of yours, Dad."

Then she was out the door and down the stairs, and back out among the other freshmen engaged in the frenzy of college: day one.

On her way back to the dorm, Jenna got a few wary "hellos" from some of the other freshmen. A bunch of guys were already on the quad doing their "guy" thing: posturing. They tossed a Frisbee around, trying to outperform one another in acrobatics. Some of them actually had their shirts off, when Jenna thought it was cold enough for a jacket. She wished she had taken her father up on his offer to lend her one.

It occurred to her, not for the first time, that having him around—or more accurately, having his *car* around—might come in handy. In fact, she could send him out to get the wood she and Yoshiko would need for their bookshelf/entertainment center. Her books—the Laurie Kings and Stephen Kings, the Larry McMurtrys and James Lee Burkes—needed a home.

"Gotta love Dad's car," she muttered happily to herself, as she walked up the front steps of Sparrow Hall.

Inside, a guy who was definitely an upperclassman spotted her, and smiled. He was pretty cute, and Jenna smiled back, but not too much. It was rough business, striking that perfect balance between friendly and flirty, but she was up to it.

"Did you get one of these?" He held up a fat manila envelope.

"That would depend on what 'one of these' is," she replied.

Maybe I do want to be a flirt, she thought.

He laughed. "The Felbers forgot to give a lot of the freshmen their orientation packages when they picked up their keys."

"Then yes," Jenna answered. "I'm one of the lost sheep."

"Nice to meet you, sheep. I'm Jack Counihan, and here's your kit."

She took it, and started toward the stairs, smiling to herself. Jack was an upperclassman, yeah. She guessed a junior, at least. But what was better was that he wasn't like any of the guys she'd gone to high school with. Sure, he seemed cocky. Boys generally were. At least the ones unafraid to speak to girls were. But he seemed confident and intelligent and respectful, too.

All that and an education, too, she thought. *College rocks.*

Jenna couldn't believe how happy she was. Despite her mother's assurances, she'd been positive that terror would have set in by now. But so far she was just enjoying herself. Her job here was to learn, which was amazing. Four years of room and board, with nobody to answer to but herself, and no expectations from anyone except that she learn something.

"Cool," she said, and pushed through the door into the third-floor hallway.

It was chaos.

In the brief hours that she had been gone, the freshman army had descended upon Sparrow Hall. Most of the doors, particularly on the guys' side, were decorated with pictures, posters, bulletin boards, and signs for particular brands of beer. A lot of them were open, some because their occupants were still moving in, and some just because they wanted to be social. Social included pumping various musical styles and sounds out into the hallway at loud volumes, playing pickup basketball in the corridor, and swearing loudly at each other.

She checked the guys out. Couldn't help it. Most of them were average guys, no different from Timmy Hargitay or Steve Dunlap back home. Decent looking, but not heart-stopping. There were a few quiet ones, too.

As she neared the common area, Jenna heard someone shout "Hey!"

She glanced up into the most perfect face she had ever seen, just before he nearly knocked her over.

"Whoa!"

"Oh, man, sorry," said the perfect face. "I just had to catch someone, but . . ." He studied her, tilted his head to one side, and smiled. "It can wait."

His skin was a dark brown, his chin and cheekbones

strong, and his eyes were so expressive that they seemed to smile even when he didn't. He stuck out his hand.

"Damon Harris," he said. "And you're . . ."

"Oh. Jenna Blake." She shook his hand. "Nice to meet you."

"You don't know me yet," Damon said.

Jenna grinned. Raised an eyebrow. "Not yet."

She moved on. There were a couple of other really cute guys, but she was busy appreciating Damon in her mind. *Bookmark that page,* she thought, and then moved on, physically and mentally.

As Jenna passed through from the boys' side—she'd come up the steps on that side of the building—and into the common area, she realized that the little study circle was going to become no-man's-land. It was where male and female met, in love and war. Very little studying was likely to get done there. Already a couple was kissing furiously in the common area. Jenna couldn't tell whether they were saying goodbye, or hello, but they were pretty emphatic about whichever it was.

On the girls' side, things were a little different. Still lots of music. No basketball. Instead, there was gossip raging in several rooms, while most of the girls she saw through open doors were hanging up clothes or otherwise decorating their rooms.

Then she noticed that the door to 311—her room—also stood open. A thrill of excitement ran through her and she took a deep breath before turning to look into her room. The first thing she saw were the plants:

half a dozen leafy green potted things, including two so monstrous that they would have to sit on the floor like furniture. Jenna blinked in surprise. It never would have occurred to her to bring plants to the dorm. Her mother loved plants, but she'd always thought of it as, well, a grown-up kind of thing.

Of course, she was a "grown-up" now, wasn't she?

Jenna stepped into her dorm room and glanced around.

No Yoshiko.

"Can I help you?"

She spun and found herself face-to-face with a questioning glance from a pretty girl holding a pitcher of water.

"Yoshiko?" she asked.

The other girl smiled. "Jenna!" she said excitedly. "You were, like, the invisible woman or something. Your stuff was here, but . . . I've been waiting for you to show up forever!"

Yoshiko put down the pitcher and gave her an unexpected hug. Hesitating only a moment, Jenna returned it.

"We are going to have *the* coolest year!" Yoshiko declared as she stepped back.

Jenna tilted her head. "An optimist. Gotta like that," she said, even as she gazed around, taking in the things that Yoshiko had added to the room. Besides her stereo equipment, which for the moment was stacked in one corner, and the plants, there was a huge poster of Hawaii and, much to Jenna's relief, the phone and answering machine Yoshiko had promised.

She glanced at the poster again, wondering how Yoshiko had gotten it to hang.

"In case you get homesick?" Jenna asked, gesturing toward the poster.

She knew from their summer correspondence that Yoshiko had been born in Japan but lived almost her entire life on the island of Oahu in Hawaii.

"No, it's just nice to look at," Yoshiko said. Then she frowned a bit. "Is it okay? I mean, do you hate it?"

Jenna laughed. "No! This is *our* room, Yoshiko. Together. I've never shared a room, so it should be an adventure."

Yoshiko smiled. "Great. I get to be your test subject."

"Exactly," Jenna agreed. "Really, though, as long as you don't snore too loud, I just know it's going to rock."

"I'm glad we've been e-mailing. I think it made coming here easier. I was a little afraid," Yoshiko said, as if she were in confession. "And, boy, you weren't kidding when you said you liked to read. I've never seen so many books. And you never told me you were so into puzzles and all those brainteasers and stuff."

Jenna looked up, saw that Yoshiko was looking at the top of her desk. Jenna had half a dozen hunks of plastic on her desk that were actually complex puzzles, children of the Rubik's Cube. Yoshiko picked up a multicolored puzzle shaped like a snake, with dozens of interlocking pieces.

"That's a hard one," Jenna told her. "They help me clear my mind when I need to focus on homework or whatever, and I play with them a lot when I'm on-line."

Yoshiko put the puzzle down, and finally noticed the manila envelope in Jenna's hands.

"Oh, hey," the other girl said, "have you looked at that stuff? It looks like they've got us completely swamped tomorrow."

Jenna walked toward the bunk beds, then paused. "Top or bottom?"

"Either is cool," Yoshiko said sincerely.

"Yeah, but which do you want?" Jenna urged.

"I guess the top."

"Top it is," Jenna said with a grin, then dumped the manila envelope out on the lower bunk.

She sifted through a lot of paperwork about Somerset and about orientation, noticed the schedule of events for the following day, and looked up at Yoshiko.

"Do we have to attend all of these things?" she asked.

Yoshiko smiled. "It's college," she said. "My guess is, we don't *have* to do anything. But I'll probably go to most of it, especially the president's speech and the reception in the alumni hall."

Jenna nodded, then picked up a thick book with the school's logo, a rearing horse, on the cover. All of Somerset's sports teams were called the Colts, and instead of something silly like Somersetters, the student body had come to be referred to that way as well.

The book contained pictures, names, and vital infor-

mation about all the students in the incoming freshman class. When she got to her own picture, she
shrieked in horror and flipped the page. Her high
school yearbook photo had not been the best shot
ever taken of her.

"Let me see," Yoshiko insisted.

Instead, Jenna looked up *Kitsuta, Yoshiko,* and realized hers wasn't the only unflattering picture in the
book.

"Your hair looks better shorter," Jenna told her,
and Yoshiko beamed.

They talked and arranged their room until they realized it was almost six o'clock. Which meant dinnertime. And since the dining halls were only open
from five to six-thirty, they knew they had to hurry.

The closest D.H. was in the basement of Keates
Hall. As they walked from their dorm, Jenna heard
sirens in the distance. She wasn't sure if they were
police or ambulance sirens, but she figured she'd have
to get used to it, what with the Somerset Medical
Center so close.

When they walked into Keates, the dining hall was
packed with lost-looking kids Jenna assumed were
freshmen. But there were also a lot more students
who looked like upperclassmen than she had expected.
Some of them must have arrived early. Then she realized that, even if they couldn't move into their dorms,
a lot of them probably had off-campus housing.

The food wasn't anything special. Certainly not a
promising preview of things to come. Breaded fish or
beef stroganoff. Jenna went with the fish. She figured

it would be harmless, and relatively tasteless, and it was both. The potatoes that came along with it were pretty awful, however, and she went back to get french fries instead.

She and Yoshiko had managed to find an empty table near the long row of windows at the back of the room, which was a surprise, since so many people seemed to be coming in late. They were still coming in at six-thirty, and the sweet, fiftysomething woman who was checking meal cards let a bunch of latecomers through before closing off the line. Jenna saw the R.A., Jack Counihan, and gave him a little wave. He waved back, but she didn't have any sense that he recognized her.

Most of the tables were full, and Jenna got up to get some more soda. When she got back, Yoshiko was picking at cold french fries.

"We might need to make a run to the store for some snacks," Jenna said. "What if we get the munchies at, like, midnight?"

"Good point. Wish I had a car here."

"My father has a car," Jenna said, a small smile on her face.

"Your father lives around here?"

Jenna rolled her eyes. "He's a professor, actually."

"No way, why didn't you tell me that?"

"I don't know. It's kind of weird, I guess. But yeah."

"Professor Blake, huh? I'll watch out for him."

"Not Blake, actually," Jenna said, growing a bit uncomfortable. "He and my mom split a long time ago, and she went back to her maiden name. My dad's Frank Logan."

Yoshiko's eyes went wide. "I have him! Already! I'm taking Fundamentals of Law as one of my electives."

"Oh, God," Jenna sighed. "Well, if he's a slave driver, don't take it out on me."

They laughed together, and were chatting about other classes when a tall, thin blond kid came up with a tray weighed down by a pile of beef stroganoff on a plate next to a stack of french fries, two small dishes of chocolate pudding, and two cups of Coke.

"Excuse me, do you mind if I sit down?" he asked, with a slow Southern drawl. "There aren't a lot of other seats, and . . ."

He shrugged carefully, so as not to upset the huge meal on his tray. Jenna laughed. The kid looked like, well, a kid. He had a very boyish face, and barely looked old enough to be in college at all. But he made up for that with perfect hair and big blue eyes.

"Sure, have a seat," Jenna replied.

She was about to turn back to Yoshiko when the kid slid his tray onto the table, and said, "Wow, thanks. That's real nice of you. I was supposed to meet my sister here but she took off with some of her friends and left me hanging."

With a laugh, Jenna looked back at him. The guy's slow Southern drawl had been replaced by an excited, rapid-fire stream of words, only slightly colored by his accent.

"So," she said, mostly because he seemed to be

waiting for some kind of response. "What's your name?"

"Hunter. Hunter LaChance," he replied.

"Of course it is," Jenna said, raising an eyebrow at such a gentleman's name for such a gangly, baby-faced guy. "I'm Jenna Blake. This is Yoshiko Kitsuta."

Yoshiko seemed a little uncomfortable, which Jenna thought was interesting. She was very up, very open and friendly. *Just not around guys, apparently.* Yoshiko glanced shyly at Hunter as she said, "Nice to meet you."

"You too!" Hunter said excitedly. "So, where are you guys living?"

"Sparrow Hall," Jenna offered. "We're on the third floor. It's a little crazy already."

"No kidding," Hunter said. "I'm right down the hall!"

Of course you are, Jenna thought, but smiled at Hunter. He seemed like a nice guy, but his enthusiasm was making her tired just from listening to him.

Still, it might not be bad to have him down the hall. At least I'll know someone besides my roomie.

After dinner, the three of them went back to the dorm. Jenna met a lot of other people, but they seemed to drift in and out of the central conversation she was having with Hunter and Yoshiko. They never did get snacks, and Jenna promised herself they'd go to the store the next day.

By the time they kicked Hunter out of their room, it was two in the morning. Jenna and Yoshiko talked a little while before falling asleep at last.

*   *   *

It was just before eight o'clock when Detectives Audrey Gaines and Danny Mariano entered Somerset Medical Center. Visiting hours were almost over, but they showed their badges to the nurse who tried to turn them away, and kept walking.

"What room is this nutjob in?" Danny asked.

"The nutjob is named Nicholas Garson, Daniel," Audrey said grimly. "Room 619, I think."

Danny glanced at Audrey. *I think?* Danny was thirty-one, Audrey forty-four. They'd been partners three years, and she'd taught him a great deal of what he knew about being a detective. As a woman, and a black woman at that, she'd had to deal with a lot of harsh reality as she came up in the ranks—even in a second-tier city like Somerset—and it had toughened her up. They were friends, as well as partners. He had a great deal of respect for Audrey.

But "I think" made it sound like a guess, and he was sure it wasn't that. Audrey Gaines never simply guessed. She knew, or she didn't know, that was it. Dealing with the people who wanted to see her fail had made her certain never to offer information unless she knew she was correct. It also made her a very good cop.

"Something bothering you, Audrey?" he asked.

She was always tough. But tonight she was grimmer than usual.

"Trying to quit smoking," Audrey said.

Danny laughed at that. "Again?"

She glared at him. "I'll do it this time."

"I hope you do," Danny said. "But quickly. Whenever you're trying to quit you get cranky."

41

Audrey smiled at that.

Gotcha! Danny thought.

They got off the elevator on the sixth floor, and heard screaming. With barely a glance at one another, they were moving. Danny unholstered his service weapon and gripped it with both hands, moving sideways down the corridor. A lot of people were yelling, and they rounded a corner to see three orderlies trying to tear a young-looking guy with a cast on his right arm off a nurse.

He was choking her to death.

The man was bleeding from his eyes, nose, and ears, and there was blood on his chin. The nurse's white uniform had blood spattered all over it, but Danny didn't think it was hers.

"Police officers!" Audrey shouted, leveling her gun at the man, despite the orderlies crowded around him. "Let the woman go, now!"

It was like they weren't even there.

"Oh God, he's killing her!" someone yelled.

Danny holstered his gun and went into the tangle of orderlies. They were choking the man, battering at his arms, but still he wouldn't let go. There was no time to think about it, just time to act. He kicked the man in the armpit as hard as he could. The patient lost his grip, and the orderlies wrestled him to the ground.

"What do you want to bet he's our guy," Audrey said, coming up beside him and holstering her weapon.

Several doctors were checking on the nurse, who seemed to be able to breathe all right.

"What the hell?" one of the orderlies muttered.

Danny and Audrey turned to see the patient, the

lunatic attacker they assumed was the man they'd come to question, start to jerk and shake violently.

"He's having some kind of seizure," Audrey said.

"Ya think?" Danny asked, and ignored her withering glance.

The man—Nicholas Garson, if he were indeed their perp—shook so hard that his head slapped the floor, and Danny heard a crack. Still he kept shaking, arms and legs flying around. Blood streamed from his ears, nose, and eyes, and dripped out of the corners of his mouth. It was all the orderlies could do to try to hold him down.

"Out of the way!" a woman shouted, and Danny assumed she was a doctor.

Then the "nutjob" stopped. Just stopped moving.

The doctor knelt next to the man and began shouting instructions Danny couldn't make any sense of, though it was clear she was calling for some kind of drugs. He noticed that when she got a bit of the man's blood on her hand, she flinched.

He didn't like that.

He liked it even less when she spun and looked at the orderlies. "Go scrub down, right now!" she snapped. "Anyone who got his blood on you, scour yourselves."

"Is that Nicholas Garson?" Danny asked.

"It was," said the doctor.

The man was dead.

"What is it?" Audrey asked, flashing her badge at the doctor. "What killed him?"

The doctor looked at her, then looked back at the dead man. "Nothing I've ever seen before. I just hope to God it isn't contagious."

c h a p t e r   3

By the time Jenna and Yoshiko managed to drag themselves out of their bunks, they'd missed several of the morning's orientation events, including a breakfast with the history department that Yoshiko had really wanted to attend.

"I can't believe I overslept!" Yoshiko said anxiously, dropping down from her bunk. "I haven't gotten up after eight o'clock in years."

She looked very rumpled, but very much awake, her eyes quite serious as she rushed around the room, grabbing her robe, a towel, soap, and shampoo. "Wish I could say the same," Jenna replied, her eyelids threatening to shut again.

She stifled a huge yawn and crawled out of bed. "All right," she said. "I guess I'm coming, too."

Her room key was on a little rubber chain that looked like a phone cord, and she pulled it around her wrist before grabbing her own things and following Yoshiko out into the hallway.

College lesson one, Jenna thought. *Mom's not here to wake you up if you don't set the alarm clock.*

"Morning, Jenna," said a deep voice.

She looked up into Damon Harris's face. Her eyes widened. Super-aware that she must look awful, Jenna mumbled hello and kept walking, not daring to turn around to see if Damon was watching her.

When she and Yoshiko pushed into the girls' bathroom, Jenna chuckled to herself.

"I should just die now," she said.

Yoshiko smiled. "You like him?"

"Did you *see* him?" she asked. Then she looked in the mirror and groaned. "God, do you see *me?*"

A toilet flushed, and a moment later one of the bathroom stalls opened. Jenna and Yoshiko both glanced around to see a tall blond guy emerging from the stall in his boxer shorts and a T-shirt.

"Hello, isn't this the girls' bathroom?" Jenna asked, a little wigged.

The guy looked at her as though she were crazy. "You're a freshman, aren't you?" he asked.

Jenna glanced away, pulling her robe around her, and the guy kind of chuckled.

"My girlfriend, Kim Delaney, is on this floor. This bathroom's a lot closer than the one on the other side of the building."

"The *boys'* bathroom," Jenna reminded him.

"Only in name," the guy said, and stuck out his hand. "I'm Pete McHugh. I suspect we'll meet again."

Jenna shook his hand, mainly because she didn't know what else to do. Then Pete was gone, the door swinging shut behind him, and Jenna looked over to see that Yoshiko's eyes were still wide with astonishment. She was shy around guys to begin with, never mind sharing a bathroom with them.

"That's going to take some getting used to," Jenna said.

"Oh, yeah," Yoshiko replied, nodding. She leaned in and turned on the water in the nearest shower stall. "Bad enough we get to walk that hallway every morning for the rest of the year. But in here?"

Jenna sighed, shook her head, and turned on her own shower.

It was going to be a long day.

Before they left the dorm, Jenna used a pay phone to call her father. When she told him she just had too much to do to have lunch, he sounded a bit disappointed, but she made quick plans to stop by his house after her meeting with Dr. Slikowski, which her father told her was scheduled for four o'clock that afternoon.

She also asked him, in her best "I'm your only daughter and you'd better do this for me" voice, if he would go and get the planks to make up their bookcase. He assured her he would do it that very day. Jenna was pleased. Her father had a lot of time to make up for, and she only felt a *little* bit guilty reminding him of it now and again, even if it was just in the tone of her voice.

After she hung up, the girls went downhill to the

campus center—a large tile-surfaced building with a serious Asian motif—and stood in line for more than half an hour to have photos taken for their school ID cards. In line, Jenna struck up a conversation with a guy from her floor named Sam Chin. He was very nice, though not very pleased with his roommate, Brad Oliphant. From the sound of things, the two couldn't possibly be more mismatched.

Jenna looked at Yoshiko and beamed. *I lucked out.* Even before she came to school, she'd heard horror stories about bad roommates. She sympathized with Sam, but she was also happy for herself.

"What time is the president's speech?" she asked Yoshiko.

Yoshiko didn't even have to consult her orientation program. "Two o'clock."

Jenna grimaced. "I guess I can make it, if he doesn't go on too long."

"Why, what else is happening?" Yoshiko asked.

Jenna told her about the interview she had with Dr. Slikowski, which seemed to interest her roommate quite a bit, until she got around to explaining exactly what kind of medicine Dr. Slikowski practiced.

"No way."

"Way," Jenna said, laughing, then shrugged. "Who knows? Maybe it'll be just too nasty for words. But it might be cool. It sounds kind of interesting."

"I'd faint before I even got in there," Yoshiko said.

"That could happen," Jenna answered, smiling. "I'll have to wait and see."

By the time they got their ID cards, and complained

quite loudly to each other about how bad the pictures of them were, it was nearly eleven o'clock.

"Didn't you want to go to that drama and music presentation?" Yoshiko asked.

"Yeah. Is that now?"

"About thirty seconds from now," Yoshiko confirmed. "Maybe we can get our books after lunch."

They were walking toward the bookstore now, and looked up to see a very long line, coming out the door and winding along the side of the building.

"Maybe we should come back at noon, when everyone else has gone to lunch," Jenna offered. "I don't want to miss lunch, but that's probably when the line will be the shortest."

Yoshiko brightened. "Good thinking."

"Hey, I'm not just another pretty face," Jenna announced.

"I'll say you're not," Yoshiko muttered.

Jenna turned to stare at her, but when she saw the look on her roommate's face, she realized that Yoshiko was only kidding.

"Good with the witty repartee," Jenna told her. "It's almost like you grew up around here. But you should know, once you've started with the mutual insults, it's hard to stop. It's like a drug."

"I can handle it," Yoshiko said gravely. Then, after a pause, she grinned broadly.

Jenna returned her grin. Then she glanced at her watch. "We're late."

Together, they took off down the street toward

Coleman Auditorium. They came through the doors panting and managed to find a seat in the back while the audience was being serenaded by the High C's, Somerset's female a cappella group.

"Actually," Jenna whispered to Yoshiko, "I've never had the guts to audition for a show, but I've always wanted to."

"Not me," Yoshiko said, shuddering. "I'd rather have dental surgery."

Jenna grinned, and the two of them sat through the entire presentation, as one group of upperclassmen after another, musical and theatrical and comedy as well, spoke about their organizations and performed short things they'd arranged. A tall, thin black girl named Stephanie discussed the musical theater group, Center Stage, and then announced that the fall show was going to be *The Sound of Music*.

"You should audition," Yoshiko whispered. "I love that movie."

So did Jenna. Her mother had always said it was too "saccharine," but Jenna didn't care. She watched it at least once a year. The stage show was a little different, she knew, but she'd always wanted to play Maria. She was excited, but also afraid. *One of these days, I am going to have to get over my stage fright. Maybe this is the time.*

Or . . .

"Maybe next semester."

Yoshiko shook her head. "I'm sure you'd be great, Jenna."

*   *   *

When it was over, they flowed with the crowed out of Coleman Auditorium. Most everybody seemed to be going back to their dorms or heading to lunch. Jenna and Yoshiko walked up the street toward the bookstore. They followed the brick and cement path that led to the steps between the campus center and the store, and when they reached the top, Jenna smiled.

"Told ya."

"You did," Yoshiko agreed. "You get a gold star."

The line in front of the bookstore had disappeared. Inside, it was still pretty busy, but very manageable. Jenna and Yoshiko drifted away from one another amidst the stacks and stacks of required reading. Each had a list of the books they'd be required to buy for their classes, but Jenna couldn't help noticing other interesting books, and noting which classes required them, for future reference. She ended up getting away relatively cheap, since three of her classes—Europe to 1815, Fundamentals of Biology, and Elementary Spanish II—required only one book each. There were two for her International Relations class, and a whopping seven for Continuity of American Literature, including two huge anthologies and five novels.

Jenna managed to find all the books she needed for her classes in less than half an hour. The line to pay for them took another ten minutes. After she was through, she waited for Yoshiko.

They were about to walk out when Jenna heard someone call her name. She turned and saw Hunter LaChance standing at the back of the line with a stack of books. He was with a beautiful blond girl whose wavy hair Jenna couldn't help but envy. It took her a moment, and several glances between Hunter and the girl, to realize they must be brother and sister.

"Should we wait?" Jenna asked Yoshiko.

"Why not," her roommate replied. "We can see if he wants to go to lunch. He'll probably say yes even if he's already eaten."

Jenna tilted her head and shot a questioning glance at Yoshiko.

Who rolled her eyes. "Come on, Jenna, he's majorly into you. You couldn't tell last night?"

"No," Jenna replied sharply. "And I can't tell now. He's a nice guy. That's all. Totally not my type."

"Poor Hunter," Yoshiko sighed, with a smirk. "You're going to break his heart every day for a year."

"That's me. Jenna Blake, heartbreaker."

They waited for Hunter to pay for his books. He walked over with two large bags in his hands, grinning the whole way.

"Hey, guys," he said. "Crazy day, huh?"

But Jenna wasn't paying attention to Hunter. She was smiling at the girl with him, instead. She reached out a hand.

"I'm Jenna," she said.

The other girl laughed. "Melody LaChance," she replied. "My little brother's got the accent of a Southerner, but the manners of a buffalo."

Hunter flushed and stammered a bit, trying to defend himself. Jenna chuckled at that, as Melody and Yoshiko introduced themselves to one another.

"Don't worry about it, Hunter," Jenna said. "Women are always a double-edge sword. Here you're surrounded by us, which makes you look good—particularly considering the array of beauty here—and you know we're going to crucify you every chance we get. 'Cause you're a guy, and you were born deserving it."

"I think I'm going to like you," Melody said, grinning at Jenna, her blue eyes sparkling.

"This was a mistake," Hunter grunted as they walked out the door.

Yoshiko glanced over at Jenna. "Array of beauty?"

"Okay, so I was exaggerating," Jenna said with a shrug. "Nobody else is going to say it, right? Might as well hear it from my own lips."

With a small giggle, Yoshiko said, "I can live with that."

The rest of the walk to the dining hall, the three girls teased Hunter mercilessly, Melody revealing more about her little brother than was healthy for any of them to know. Hunter seemed to get smaller and smaller as they walked, to the point where even Jenna grew uncomfortable.

"Okay," she sighed as they reached the door. "Now even I'm beginning to feel sorry for him, Melody."

"Great," Hunter said dryly. "Thanks. Just what I wanted. Pity."

"Pity is good," Melody told him. "It's better than disgust."

Yoshiko didn't say much. The wisecracking side of her personality seemed to hide away when Hunter was around. Jenna hadn't known her long enough to figure out whether it was all boys, or just Hunter, but she'd find out soon enough.

Melody, on the other hand, was supremely confident. Maybe it was because the only guy around was her little brother, but Jenna didn't think so. She was a sophomore, only a year older than the rest of them, but she had a kind of control of the conversation, and the situation, that Jenna envied. Plus, she was taller, about five foot eight, and Jenna envied her that as well. In high school, Melody was the kind of girl she might have hated. But she'd only known her forty-five minutes when she realized they were going to be friends.

The real tip-off came when, as they were eating the various substances passed off that day as food, Melody turned to her brother. "Hunter, did you notice they're doing *The Sound of Music* this semester?" she said. "You should audition."

Hunter shook his head. "I don't think so, Mel. I want to focus on classes first semester. If I do all right, maybe I'll think about doing a show next time. Besides, if you get Maria, I don't think I'd want to be Captain Von Trapp."

Jenna smiled.

"What?" Melody asked her.

"Jenna wants to audition but she's chicken," Yoshiko explained.

"I'm not chicken," Jenna protested, shooting Yoshiko a withering glance. "I just . . . it's like with Hunter. I want to focus on my academic career first."

Yoshiko gave her a dubious look, but Jenna thought, *That's my story and I'm stickin' to it.*

"Well, I hope you change your mind," Melody said. "Last year we were hurting for dedicated talent."

"I love musicals," Jenna said. "Did you see *Rent?*"

"She saw it three times," Hunter sighed and rolled his eyes. "I'm glad to say that she only tortured me with it once."

When they walked out of the dining hall, Jenna and Melody were discussing various musicals they'd seen, and then went on to movies and books. Behind them, Hunter and Yoshiko talked quietly, mostly about classes. Jenna felt a little guilty, but soon she was laughing away with Melody.

They sat together at the president's orientation address, though Melody didn't technically need to be there. They talked through most of it, Jenna whispering to Melody about her family situation, and Melody telling her about her own family, including their history with Somerset University. It had been taken for granted that she and Hunter would attend Somerset. Which, since it was such a well-respected school, was okay with her.

When the president finally finished his long-winded speech about the diversity of Somerset's student body, and all the wonderful assets the school had to offer its students—all of which Jenna had already read in mailings and the school handbook—it was three-thirty-five. Yoshiko dragged Hunter off to the alumni tea, but Jenna had to hurry in order to make her four o'clock appointment with Dr. Slikowski.

"Call me later," Melody said, scribbling her number on the back of Jenna's bookstore receipt. "We could hang out. Maybe get pizza or something. Bring Yoshiko if you want; and if you have to, you can drag Hunter along as well."

Jenna laughed at that and promised to call her later. Then she rushed back to her dorm to change her clothes, and drop off her books, all in the space of ten minutes.

Somerset Medical School was a short walk from Sparrow Hall, and the medical center was just beyond that. Other than the sprint across Carpenter Street, dodging the mixture of local, school, and hospital traffic, it was a pleasant walk on paved paths among rows of trees. There was an enormous parking lot behind the med school buildings and another behind the hospital, but the front, where they looked out over the hill and Somerset beyond, was just green, much like the campus.

When Jenna rode the elevator to the second floor, and walked down a long, busy corridor to a line of administrative offices, it was ten past four. But when she walked into Walter Slikowski's office, nobody glanced up and told her she was late. There was a young guy with olive skin and dark, curly hair working busily at a corner desk, filling out paperwork. The phone was ringing and the guy tried to ignore it before finally picking it up.

Jenna waited patiently until the guy hung up the phone, and then cleared her throat.

The guy looked up. "What can I do for you?" he asked.

"My name's Jenna Blake," she said, a bit nervous. "I had a four o'clock appointment with Dr. Slikowski."

The young man smiled amiably, then walked over and held out a hand. "Nice to meet you, Jenna. I'm Albert Dyson. I'm a pathology resident here."

"Which means almost nothing to me," Jenna said, with an apologetic look.

Dyson nodded. "I'm a doctor, but I'm doing my residency in pathology, which basically means I'm training to become a medical examiner."

"So do you do the autopsies and stuff?" she asked, feeling horribly ignorant.

"A lot of them," he replied. "Or, at least, I do a lot of the scut work. Slick is a pretty busy guy."

"Slick?" Jenna asked, her whole image of Dr. Slikowski changing from the white-haired old fogey she'd had in mind.

Dyson laughed. "Sorry. Don't let him hear you call him that, okay?"

"Deal. So he's the medical examiner here?" she asked.

"Actually, he's the chief M.E. for the whole county, as well as the chairman of the hospital's pathology department, an instructor at the school, and chief of autopsy. Not to mention the forensic pathologist for the local cops. All of which means he's pretty well stretched to the limit. If he's not performing an autopsy, he's probably on his way to one, or writing up notes, or what have you. Believe me, I'd be happy to have an extra pair of hands around."

Jenna blinked,

"Too much information, huh?" Dyson asked.

She nodded.

"You know the difference between a coroner and a medical examiner?"

"Do they even have coroners anymore?"

Dyson smiled. "Not much. Some places, the position is still called that. But a coroner is just an official, not necessarily an M.D. The medical examiner is an M.D., and a pathologist. The job entails an investigation into all sudden, suspicious, or violent deaths."

"Investigation?" Jenna asked. "Isn't that the police department's job?"

"Scientific investigation," Dyson explained. "That's the point of an autopsy. Although Dr. Slikowski does work with the police as a forensic consultant."

"So they call him in to help them solve crimes, using science," Jenna said, watching Dyson to see if she was on the tright track.

"Exactly," he said, smiling. "See. You'll pick it up quickly as you go along. But you picked a pretty bad day to start."

Then she blinked, and finally got it. "Wait a second, Dr. Dyson, I'm not starting today. I was just supposed to interview."

He laughed. "Just Dyson, please. Unless you're a patient or my mortal enemy. And I guess I'm getting ahead of myself. Why don't you have a seat and Sli—, I mean, Dr. Slikowski, will be back in a minute."

She did as he suggested, and nearly twenty minutes passed in relative silence before the doorknob turned, clicked, and the door was shoved open from the outside. Jenna looked up expectantly, but for a moment, no one came in.

Then a man in a wheelchair glided into the room, maneuvered his wheels so that he could give the door a hard shove to close it, and then started toward Dyson.

Jenna blinked. He was a thin, good-looking man, about fortyish, with well-groomed, graying hair and wire-rim glasses on his nose. He wasn't wearing a lab coat, but he did have an identification tag hanging from the pocket of his Oxford shirt.

"Dr. Dyson," he began. Then he obviously noticed that Dyson's eyes had strayed behind him, and he spun his chair to face Jenna.

He allowed a small smile to cross his lips, as though he felt he needed to prove that he *could* smile, and then it was gone.

"Ah, you must be Jenna," the man said.

Surprised, Jenna paused a moment before asking, "Dr. Slikowski?"

He nodded. "Of course. I'm sorry, but I've just had an administrative meeting that lasted far too long. Dr. Dyson and I have an autopsy to perform, and then I have a class to teach tonight. Perhaps another time?"

Jenna was about to agree, when Dyson walked over. "Why don't you let her come along, Dr. Slikowski?" he suggested. "You can interview her during the autopsy. If she's still in the room when we're done, you'll know if she can do the job."

"Uh, that's okay," Jenna said doubtfully, her face growing pale. "I don't mind coming back."

Despite Dyson's amused tone, and Jenna's response, Slikowski was gravely serious as he considered this suggestion, his eyes narrowing as he did.

"Excellent idea, Dr. Dyson," he decided. "If it's all right with you, young lady?"

Young lady? Jenna thought. *Is this guy forty-five, or eighty-five?*

She swallowed hard. "Okay."

As she followed Slick and Dyson down the corridor to the elevators, the M.E. struck up a conversation with her without turning around.

"You know, Jenna, your father called at precisely the right time," he said. "I hadn't been looking for a pathology assistant, but Dr. Dyson has been badgering me to do so."

"I was sort of wondering about that," Jenna confessed. "I mean, I thought there would be medical students applying for the job, all that sort of thing."

Dyson glanced back at her, let her catch up a bit, and shook his head with disdain. "There isn't much actual medicine involved in being a path assistant," he explained. "Most medical students wouldn't take the time, unless pathology was their long-term goal, and even then, they'd probably wait and intern in path instead. It's pretty much scut work."

"Indeed," Dr. Slikowski agreed. "But if you have an interest in medicine, pathology or not, it's an excellent way to get your feet wet, so to speak. Despite what the average Somerset medical student might think."

Jenna smiled at Dr. Slikowski politely as he glanced back at her. She wondered why he was confined to a wheelchair and was curious to see how the wheelchair-bound doctor could perform an autopsy. Then she realized that he probably had pathology residents perform most of the procedures.

They rode the elevator down to the basement level. Jenna began to get an odd feeling in the pit of her stomach, a kind of chill that crept up inside her until even her scalp tingled. When they stepped off the elevator, the first thing she noticed was how cold it felt. And, worse than the cold, there was an antiseptic smell that seemed to be there to try to make people forget they were walking toward the morgue. But in the quiet and glaring artificial light, the smell was more of a reminder than anything else.

Dyson gave her a kind of play-by-play.

"All of the hospital's deceased end up down here, before moving on to whatever their final destination is. And DOAs from the local area are brought here as well."

"But not every person who dies is autopsied, right?" Jenna asked, growing curious.

"No, thank God. We'd have to quadruple our staff for that. Still, it's more than you'd think. It isn't just murder victims or people who die suspiciously. Anyone who dies a violent death receives an autopsy as standard operating procedure."

Jenna frowned. "Even someone who died in, like, a car accident or something?"

"Seems odd, doesn't it?" Slick noted. "But think a moment. Someone who dies in a car accident might have been driving under the influence of a foreign substance, or had a heart attack behind the wheel. The cause of death may seem obvious, but the reality may be less so."

When they reached the morgue, Dyson went inside, while Slick led Jenna to a large room filled with gleaming metal equipment, scales, a camera, a computer, and a large metal autopsy table with a huge vent above it. The autopsy room. There was an acid stink in the room unlike anything Jenna had ever smelled before. Immediately, her nostrils began to burn and her eyes teared up a little.

"God, what's that smell?" she asked, horrified, her eyes burning now, too.

"Formaldehyde," Dr. Slikowski replied. "It burns the eyes and mucous membranes for a bit, but you get used to it after a while."

A wisecrack floated to Jenna's lips, but she held it back. She was here to interview for a job—weird as it was—and she didn't think sarcasm would score too many points.

A few moments later, Dyson returned with a gurney, upon which lay a white-sheet–covered corpse.

Oh God. Maybe this wasn't such a good idea.

Despite her hesitancy, however, Jenna stayed put. There was something captivating about all of this. She was surprised that Dyson could move the body onto the autopsy table himself, but he managed with some maneuvering. Clearly, he'd done it before.

When he pulled the sheet off, grinning at Jenna, he looked like a magician particularly proud of his latest trick. *Toto, I don't think we're in Kansas anymore,* Jenna thought. Her stomach churned as she stared at the dead man, whose body looked bloated and pale, except in the dark areas under the skin on the backs of his legs and on his back, as if that entire side of his body were one huge blood blister.

Jenna breathed through her mouth. It didn't smell. Not really. But she felt she had to.

"Toxicology said nothing airborne?" Slick asked Dyson, who nodded. Slick shrugged. "Still, let's have masks."

The two doctors put on masks and rubber gloves, and then Dyson brought a mask over to Jenna.

"Better put it on," he said.

He used a large camera setup that looked like a dental X-ray machine to take some photographs of the corpse, then moved back and forth, measuring the dead man from head to foot.

Dr. Slikowski moved the arms of his wheelchair out of the way and used a remote control to lower the autopsy table to a position just above his knees and began to examine the body. Then he turned on a tape recorder that hung above the table.

"Subject, Nicholas Garson; autopsy 433-958-01," he began. "Caucasian male. Age thirty-four. Height, five feet ten inches; weight, one hundred ninety-seven pounds. Contusions reflecting struggle with hospital orderlies. Birthmark on inner left thigh. Abdominal scar from apparent appendix removal. No other external markings."

He reached out and Dyson handed him a scalpel. *Here we go*, Jenna thought, swallowing hard. Dr. Slikowski inserted the blade into the dead man's chest, and began to slice. Jenna tried not to let her expression show what she was feeling inside, but her stomach was a bit queasy, and she shivered as the blade glided through flesh.

Just when Jenna thought Dr. Slikowski had forgotten all about their interview, he glanced up at her.

"So, Miss Blake," he said, as he returned to his work. "Tell me about yourself."

chapter 4

As Dr. Slikowski sliced open Nicholas Garson's corpse, Jenna could only stare. He made a long incision in the torso shaped like a Y, then used his gloved fingers to peel the man's flesh back like he was tearing the wrapping off a Christmas present.

"Jenna? You still with us?" Dyson asked.

She blinked. "Huh? Oh, yeah."

Slick frowned and looked down inside the man's body, and Jenna shivered.

"Well, I'm eighteen. I scored a 1380 combined on my SATs . . ." She looked at Dr. Slikowski, wondering if he was even paying attention. "You know my father, and my mom is a doctor in Natick."

The M.E. glanced up at her from his wheelchair, nodded slowly. "April Blake," he said. "Yes, I've known your mother for years."

That surprised Jenna. Her dad hadn't mentioned it. But she figured it only gave her a better chance at getting a job here. A thought which made her back-track and wonder if she really wanted a job here.

Which was when Slick backed his wheelchair up, glanced at Dyson, and said, "Remove the ribs and sternum please, Dr. Dyson."

Jenna's eyes widened as Dyson produced a large set of what looked like industrial shears or bolt cutters, but in reality, turned out to be a kind of bone scissors, with which he could clip the ribs clean through.

Dyson bent over the corpse, and soon he was snipping through the dead man's rib cage. It didn't look easy. It occurred to her that Slick—who seemed to hate to delegate—had Dyson do this part of the autopsy because, though he might be able to reach the corpse in his wheelchair, he couldn't get the leverage necessary for something so forceful.

Jenna stared and said nothing.

"Please continue," Slick suggested.

"Go on, Jenna," Dyson said. "Most people your age would have already run from the room. You're doing well."

She shrugged, and then she told them about her interest in medicine and her concern about her patients, as well as her hatred of blood. She also told them she didn't know exactly what she wanted to do with her life.

"Indeed," Slick agreed, as he reached into Nicholas Garson's guts and began removing organs one at a time, handing them to Dyson to be weighed.

Then Dr. Slikowski leaned forward in his chair and peered very carefully into the chest cavity.

"No signs of internal bleeding," he noted for the tape recorder. "No abdominal ascites, no unusual fluid in the chest cavity at all. Dr. Dyson will be handling the dissection of organs, but a cursory examination reveals no obvious tumors, nor anything else unusual."

Jenna felt her stomach lurch as Dyson removed the intestines in a mass of long, gray-white coils. But it wasn't bothering her as much as she'd expected it would. In fact, as she listened to Dr. Slikowski's commentary, she became gradually less disgusted and more . . . interested.

"Enough about your future, Jenna," Slick said pointedly. "Let's talk about your present. I want to know what Jenna's like. What do you do with your spare time?"

"What spare time?" she asked, rolling her eyes a little. Then she said, "I read. A lot. I play the piano, but not, like, for people or anything. I'd like to do a play or a show sometime. I spend too much time on the computer, especially when I need to research something for school . . ."

She paused. Stared at the dead man.

"Can I ask *you* something?"

Dr. Slikowski raised his eyebrows and regarded her with a questioning glance. "Please," he said, nodding for her to go on.

"Well, it doesn't seem like there's anything wrong with this guy. He's kind of young, right? So, how did he die?"

Dyson shook his head, but said nothing as he continued weighing organs.

Slick tilted his head and narrowed his eyes, studying her. "How did he die?" the man repeated. "Well, that's what we're here to find out, isn't it?"

Jenna nodded.

The M.E. turned to Dyson. "Let's do a full tox screen. Get the stomach contents and a urine sample and get them off to the lab as well."

With a nod, Dyson continued about his business. He arranged the organs on a stainless steel scale and looked at them a second. Jenna assumed he'd have to go back to them. She realized that, technically, the autopsy had just begun.

"Do you want to do a vitreous?" Dyson asked.

Dr. Slikowski paused and glanced up at Jenna. He seemed to be considering something. "You might want to step out for this, Jenna," he finally said. "I won't hold it against you if you do. Even the folks with cast-iron stomachs get a bit squeamish about sampling vitreous."

Jenna had no idea what he was talking about, but she was pretty certain if she excused herself from any part of the autopsy, she could probably kiss the job good-bye. And sometime between the cracking of the dead man's rib cage and the removal of his intestines, she'd decided that all of this really disgusting, revolting stuff was actually pretty fascinating. There was a mystery here, and that was what did it.

She wanted to know how he died. She wanted to find out. It seemed vitally important to her, and she knew that somewhere out in the world, there were others to whom it was important. Maybe his family. Maybe the cops. Someone. A mystery.

"No," she said. "I'll stay."

Dyson chuckled, but Slick just shrugged. He wheeled back to a metal table full of drawers, opened one, and withdrew a long hypodermic wrapped in plastic. He removed the plastic, arranged the hypo in his hand, and after some fiddling, attached a long, mean-looking needle.

Jenna's eyes went wide.

With great concentration, Dr. Slikowski brought the point of the needle up to the man's face. He used his left hand to pull back the corpse's eyelid, and Dyson taped it open. Jenna hated that, having the man's eye open. But she hated what happened next much more.

Slick jabbed the long needle deep into the dead man's eyeball.

Jenna gasped, stomach roiling, and put a hand to her mouth. Dyson glanced up at her.

"Gross, huh?" he asked. "Your eyes are filled with vitreous fluid. We can test it for electrolytes and other things, including the presence of toxicity."

"My God, that's disgusting," Jenna whispered, feeling as though she had somehow failed in her interview.

But how could she have known that she would be seeing something like this? Answer: she couldn't. And, come to think of it, Dr. Slikowski couldn't expect her to sit through all this and not react at least a little bit.

Carefully, Slick began to draw the plunger back,

and at first, a milky fluid flowed into the long hypo. Then there was a bit of red, of blood, and then just nothing.

With a frown, Slick cursed under his breath.

"What is it?" Dyson asked, the smile disappearing from his face.

"I'm not sure," Slick replied.

He sat back and stared at the needle thrust into Nicholas Garson's eye. Then he seemed to shrug a bit, and reached for it. He tried to remove it, but the needle did not slide out easily. Slick raised an eyebrow and gave another, more forceful tug.

The dead man's eye popped out of its socket, skewered on the needle. It was shriveled like a grape and all but disconnected from the optic nerve, attached by a thin, frayed bit of muscle and nothing else. Then, even that tore away.

With a gasp, Jenna turned away. She shook a bit, felt as though she might throw up, and wanted to cry. It was stupid. She was eighteen years old, and not a kid anymore. She barely knew her father, and certainly didn't know Dr. Slikowski, but she felt as though she had let them both down.

When she turned to see that Dyson had turned an ugly shade of green and had covered his mouth, and that the medical examiner himself had pushed his wheelchair back from the autopsy table with the eyeball-impaling needle still in his hand, she felt a little better.

"I take it that's not supposed to happen," she croaked.

"No," Slick replied. "No, it's not."

Dyson recovered enough to offer Slick a dish into which the needle and eye were deposited. Then he reached up and moved a large blazing light on its metal arm over the dead man's face.

Jenna stared in horror as Slick began to cut into the man's forehead, just below the hairline, with a scalpel.

"I owe you an apology, Miss Blake," Dr. Slikowski said. "I was a bit flip with you when you asked how this man died. It was, most certainly, an odd death. His reported behavior had been—shall we say—erratic. He experienced several violent, even homicidal, episodes. And when he finally died in convulsions, he was hemorrhaging from ears, eyes, nose, and mouth."

"So there's something wrong with his brain?"

"It would seem," Slick replied.

"Then why didn't you start there?" Jenna asked, perplexed.

Dyson nodded. "That's a good question. Actually, there's a kind of pattern we follow during an autopsy, and it's rarely deviated from."

"Rarely deviated from," Slick added, "because if one assumes anything at all about the cause of death, it is increasingly probable that something else, something vital, will be overlooked."

"At first they'd thought it might be something contagious, a virus or supergerm," Dyson added.

Jenna stiffened. "You mean like ebola or something?"

"Yeah. But don't worry. We did some prep tests in the path lab before starting the autopsy. There were some oddities in the blood sample, but nothing that looked dangerous."

She stared at him. "Great. How comforting."

When Slick turned on the bone saw—what looked like a small dentist's drill with a tiny buzz saw on the end—Jenna jumped, her heart pumping wildly. With the skull exposed, the skin clipped back, Slick went to work cutting off the top of the man's head.

All that hemorrhaging, Jenna thought. *Got to be something wrong with his brain.* Then, a moment later, *Gotta be something wrong with mine to be standing here watching this stuff.*

Dr. Slikowski removed the cap of the dead man's skull, swung the light around, and stared. She couldn't see his face very well with his mask on, but his eyes were filled with astonishment, and maybe a little fear.

"Dear God," he whispered. "Dyson, take a look at this."

"Walter?" Dyson asked, furrowing his brow, the first time he'd used the M.E.'s given name.

Slick moved his chair back to allow Dyson room to peer into the open skull.

They seemed to have forgotten her. But Jenna couldn't help herself. She began to move toward the autopsy table, slowly. If these two men were horrified by what they saw, how could she even think to look? *But I have to. I have to see.* The suspense was too much.

At the table, she sidled around to one side, and then looked down where the light was gleaming off the dead man's brain. She'd never seen a person's brain, other than in horror movies, but she knew it didn't look right. It was bluish, and swollen, like it might explode. But what was worse was that Nicholas Garson's brain looked like a huge sponge. There were holes of various sizes through the whole thing, as though it were Swiss cheese.

"Oh, man," she muttered.

"Walter, look!" Dyson shouted, and took two quick steps back to bump against a metal table, rattling the drawers.

Dr. Slikowski looked. Jenna looked also. They hadn't noticed at first, because the things were so small. But inside the holes and around the edges, dozens of tiny, maggotlike creatures crawled.

Dr. Dyson threw up into a steel sink across the room.

Jenna gagged, but only stared, wide-eyed. Slick turned to her and said, "I think you should leave. Wait for me back in my office, please, and don't discuss this with anyone. I won't be long."

Numbed with revulsion by what she'd seen, Jenna nodded and sleepwalked out of the autopsy room.

"Get *out!*" Yoshiko yelled, her eyes wide.

"No, you get out," Jenna replied. "I swear it's true."

She sat on the floor, her back against the bunk beds, her knees drawn up under her chin. She stared at the television, barely registering what was on. *Apparently not Must-See TV*, she thought idly.

Yoshiko spun her desk chair around, dragged it over, and plopped down, staring at Jenna.

"So what was it? What did the doctor say? I mean, are you . . ." she said, and then paused, blinking, as she leaned back a bit. "Is it contagious?"

Jenna shook her head. "They tested my blood right there. Their own, too. Whatever it is—and believe me when I say whatever they tell people later on, they have no freakin' clue what it is—you can't get it through the air, or even by touch."

She looked at Yoshiko, narrowed her eyes. "Can you keep a secret?"

Leaning forward again, Yoshiko nodded.

"Don't tell anyone," Jenna persisted. "Not even Hunter."

"Why would I tell Hunter?" Yoshiko asked, with a grimace.

Jenna shrugged. Paused. Then looked at Yoshiko intently. "I heard Dr. Slikowski tell Dr. Dyson that the way the guy's brain looked, that's what people's brains look like when they've died from that mad cow disease."

"Oh my God," Yoshiko whispered.

"Yeah," Jenna agreed, and turned to look out the window into the darkness.

Her second night at college hadn't been anywhere near as fun as her first. She'd spent hours at the hospital and returned just before eight to find Hunter and Yoshiko hanging out in her room. After half listening to them catching her up on the afternoon's orientation activities—including the little dramatization of date

73

rape the R.A.'s had put on in the lobby—she'd asked Hunter to leave, telling him she didn't feel well, and then ordered a sub from Espresso Pizza, which Melody had highly recommended for late-night junk food.

She had barely tasted it.

Eventually, with Yoshiko's prodding about how her interview with Dr. Slikowski went, Jenna had to tell her. She just needed to talk to someone about it, and she couldn't call her father. Their phone still wasn't hooked up. In fact, she'd had to go down to use the pay phone just to call Melody and say she wouldn't be able to hang out with her, and then to call for her sub. Never mind the fact that her mother's phone bill would be soaring if she had to call collect every time she wanted to talk, as she had that morning.

Jenna gazed into the night, and a small chill passed through her as she remembered the revolting sights she had seen at Somerset Medical Center earlier.

"How . . ." Yoshiko began. "I mean, how did he get it? Was it something he ate?"

Jenna glanced at her. Her mind was whirling as she stood up and went to the window. Finally, she turned to face Yoshiko, shaking her head as she tried to make sense of it all.

"While I was waiting for them to test my blood, I asked Dr. Slikowski about it," she said. "When I said it was like mad cow disease . . . well, it sort of is and sort of isn't.

"See, some of the symptoms the poor guy had before he died were kind of like that. I mean, he went spastic or whatever, and that's one of the symptoms.

And the way his brain was, all full of holes and spongy, that's similar too.

"But the violence? That was new. And Slick—that's Dr. Slikowski—he said the bleeding like that was a lot like some other diseases, but not really associated with mad cow. So it probably didn't come from something the dead guy ate."

Yoshiko just stared at Jenna, her face contorted with her horror and disgust. "Well where did all those gross *things* come from?"

Jenna nodded to herself. "That's just it, Yoshiko," she said. "The docs think the disease most likely came from those maggots, or whatever they were."

"But how did they get *in* there?"

"I don't even think I want to know," Jenna replied, shuddering.

Then she took another bite of the roast beef and provolone sub she'd gotten half an hour earlier, even as Yoshiko wrinkled her nose in distaste.

"How can you even eat?" her roommate asked.

Jenna shrugged. "I'm hungry."

"I don't know how," Yoshiko said. "Ee-ew. I guess that job's out. Looks like Alumni Telefund, huh?"

"What?" Jenna asked. "Why?"

Yoshiko looked horrified. "Don't tell me you're still thinking about working there?"

Amused by her roommate's reaction, Jenna smiled and nodded. "Of course I am. Dr. Slikowski said he was surprised I'd stayed for the whole thing. Offered me the job while he was drawing my blood, if I wanted it. After a day like today, how could I not work there? It was probably the most interesting, most exciting thing I've ever been involved with.''

Yoshiko was speechless.

When she finally fell asleep, after eleven, Jenna dreamed.

She is walking through the sterile basement corridor of Somerset Medical Center. It is dark and cold, as though the atmosphere of the morgue has spread throughout the hospital, or at least throughout the basement. Down here.

Down here among the dead.

Her mother stands just inside the elevator doors at the end of the hall. Jenna calls out to her, and terror fills her mother's face. April opens her mouth, silently shouting to her daughter and pointing. But then the elevator doors hiss closed and do not open again.

Jenna turns to look at whatever her mother was pointing at, and when she turns, she is no longer at the hospital. She is in the common area on the third floor of Sparrow Hall. Melody and Hunter and Yoshiko are there, and so are Dyson and Slick.

Slick is standing, not in his wheelchair, and he looks younger to her.

"What happened to you?" she asks him, the question she wanted to ask him when she first saw him.

He frowns, and says nothing, but she knows the answer. Nothing. Yet.

Embarrassed, she goes to the door to her room, but when she opens it, she is standing in front of her father's house. It is dark, but a single light burns in a window on the second floor.

He's left the light on for her. After all these years, he wants his little girl to come home.

Without going up the stairs or opening the door, she finds herself suddenly inside. She is aware that her clothes have changed. Somehow she'd been wearing a white lab coat before. Now she has on feetie pajamas with Tweety Birds on them, just like she wore when she was a little girl, when her father still loved her enough to stay . . .

Jenna woke up a few minutes after three in the morning, filled with sadness. It took her several seconds to realize she had been dreaming, and several more to understand that her odd dreams about her father meant nothing.

Well, nothing except that she wanted him to love her. But he did. She knew he did. But she supposed that knowing it and feeling it were two different things.

She lay back down and, eventually, began to drift off again. Just before she fell asleep, she remembered the other part of the dream. In the hospital basement, with her mother yelling to her, warning her of something down there, something that could hurt her.

Jenna didn't dream any more that night.

At dawn, Professor Mattei awoke with a nasty itch in his left ear. He stuck his finger in even before his eyes opened, and stirred it around. But the itch didn't subside.

By the time he had dragged himself to the bathroom and relieved his bladder, he was swearing loudly in Spanish and rubbing his whole ear, as if that might be enough to stop the itching.

It wasn't.

"Hijo de perra!" he snarled as he screwed his finger into his ear harder and harder.

He started slapping himself in the side of the head, growing more and more infuriated. The itch wouldn't go away.

Enraged, he picked up a can of shaving cream from on top of the sink and threw it. The can struck the shower door. The glass splintered into a spiderweb pattern of cracks, but thankfully did not shatter.

The itch stopped.

Breathing hard, Professor Mattei blinked and stared at the cracked shower door. He would have to use cold water to make sure he didn't make the glass any worse, and then have it replaced later in the day.

What was I thinking?

By breakfast, he'd forgotten all about the itch in his ear.

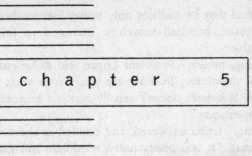

At the bottom of Memorial Steps, University Boulevard was lined with establishments that subsisted mainly on the college trade. Espresso Pizza, Jay's Deli, Video Plus, Art's Liquors, Somerset Laundromat . . . they lined the boulevard, and most of them had been there for ten, twenty, thirty years.

Paula's Bakery Café was new to the hillside area. The owner, whose name was pronounced "pow-la," had grown up in Brazil and attended Somerset herself. She had money. The first Paula's Bakery Café had opened in Boston five years earlier, and had been a huge success. It wasn't long before it became a chain, and now, as sort of a nostalgic nod to her college days, she was presiding over the grand opening of the latest Paula's, right there in Somerset.

Jenna shouldered her way through the packed house, glancing about the place for her father. It was Saturday morning, just after ten, and she was astonished to find that he had not only beaten her to their meeting place, but had somehow managed to find them a table.

"Morning, honey," Professor Logan said as he embraced his daughter. "So how are you? From what I know, Dr. Slikowski doesn't usually conduct business during an autopsy."

"I'm fine," Jenna answered, and nodded as she slid into her seat. "It was pretty nasty, no doubt. But I'm all right."

"Are you sure?" Frank prodded, trying to get Jenna to meet his gaze.

She did. With a slight grin. And she nodded again, but slowly this time. "I'm fine, Dad. Really." Then her eyes narrowed. "Why? Did Slick say something? Doesn't he think I can do it?"

Her father looked very surprised, blinked twice, and then shook his head, laughing softly. "Slick?" he asked.

Jenna paled. "Oh. Wow. Sorry. Don't tell him I said that, okay?"

Frank laughed again, rocking back in his chair, looking just as neat as always. Which was to say, not at all. "I won't mention it," he said. "But you should watch that. Nobody who wants to stay on his good side calls him Slick.

"And no, he didn't say anything other than that he's looking forward to having you there. You're supposed to start Tuesday, right?"

The waitress arrived and Jenna ordered a cappuccino and a croissant. Her father was already drinking coffee, black, but he ordered a cinnamon danish.

"So, Tuesday, yeah," Jenna agreed. "I don't have class after two on Tuesdays."

She gazed through the milling crowd. The tall, beautiful, almost Amazonian Paula was smiling broadly and chatting with several customers who were obviously old friends or acquaintances. A space opened through the crowd, and she could see out through the windows at the cars and people passing by on University Boulevard.

"Do me a favor, though," she asked her father.

He looked up at her over the rim of his coffee mug. Raised his eyebrows.

"My phone finally got turned on this morning," she said. "Of course I called Mom first."

"She doesn't want you to take the job," her father guessed.

"I don't know if it's that, so much. I think she just feels like I'm going about it the wrong way," Jenna replied.

Her father frowned. "If you wanted to be a *real* doctor. As opposed to an M.E. or forensic specialist or something else she doesn't consider to be medicine."

Jenna didn't respond. She didn't want to create an argument between her parents, but her mother wasn't about to listen to her. And she *was* going to take that job. Her mother would never hold her education over her head as a way to get her to behave in a certain way. But all things being equal, it would be much better all around if her mother approved of her choices.

"I'll talk to her," Frank said firmly.

Jenna looked at him closely. "Okay," she said. "But do us both a favor. Don't try to convince her she's wrong and you're right. Just try to get her to understand that I need to make my own decisions on things. That way she won't send out the hit squad for you."

"Again?" her father said, smiling. "That trick never works."

Jenna laughed. Then her cappuccino arrived, and they talked about more mundane things, like her new friends, and a party she planned to attend at the arts house that night. On the subject of his daughter going to a party, Frank Logan said nothing.

Good, Jenna thought. *He's not going to try to play Daddy.*

But a little part of her was disappointed, too. It would have been nice if he'd made a little bit of a fuss out of it.

"What the hell's a botfly?"

Danny Mariano glanced over at his partner and sighed. Sometimes he wished Audrey would grow a little more tact. Make that *most* of the time. Still, she was one of the best detectives he'd ever seen. Not that he was all that experienced. At thirty-one, the other detectives in their squad still called him "kid."

Behind the large desk in his neat, well-appointed office, Dr. Slikowski leaned back in his wheelchair, removed his wire-rim glasses and began to clean them with the edge of his lab coat. Danny liked the guy in spite of himself. He was probably not much more than ten years older, but Walter Slikowski acted seventy-five.

"He's just reserved," Audrey would say, any time Danny would complain about the unsmiling medical examiner.

"Or maybe he's just arrogant," Danny would always suggest.

Audrey usually glowered at him.

Today, she was too busy being cranky to glower at anyone in particular. But he couldn't blame her. Nobody was questioning what had happened in the courthouse the day Nicholas Garson had gone wacko, but Danny and Audrey needed to figure out why so they could close the book.

"A botfly is a type of insect usually found in Central America," Dr. Slikowski replied. "Apparently they are particularly numerous in the rain forests of Costa Rica. Travel brochures frequently warn tourists about them."

Danny sat up in his chair. "That makes sense," he said. "This Garson guy was a congressional aide. He'd just returned from some meeting in Costa Rica. That solves that mystery."

He was pleased, hoping to make a quick exit and be done with this nasty little case.

"Not so fast," Audrey said.

Danny sighed.

"So these botflies aren't all that uncommon," she said. "If they're carrying this disease, then why haven't we seen this kind of reaction before? I mean, the perp completely lost it, went out and out postal, and from what you've said, it turned his brains to Swiss cheese."

Dr. Slikowski frowned and cleared his throat. "I'm sure that isn't how I put it, Detective Gaines," he said. "But you are correct. I've already contacted the Centers for Disease Control, and they're sending someone up as soon as possible."

"Are we looking at a quarantine?" Danny asked.

"No. As I told you last night, whatever this disease is, we can be grateful for one thing: it isn't easily spread. If it got into the drinking water, or into our food, or if you were to ingest it in some other way, it might spread quickly. But as long as we contain Mr. Garson's corpse—keep it away from cannibals, if you will—we should be all right."

Danny blinked. Walter Slikowski had made a joke. And a pretty morbid one at that.

"Unless other people have it, too," Audrey suggested.

"Correct," Slikowski agreed. "In some ways, it is much like bovine spongiform encephalopathy, which the media would call 'mad cow disease.' It turns the brain into a spongy mass which results in a horrid neurological condition. You saw the way that man spasmed before death."

"What about the blood?" Danny asked. "He was hemorrhaging like crazy when we brought him down."

The M.E. frowned. "That's one of the major differences. As is the homicidal rage. It must be the destruction of certain parts of the brain, but that will take some time in the lab to figure out."

"If it does come up again, is there any way to cure somebody who gets this thing?"

Dr. Slikowski thought, stroking his chin, the bad office light glaring off his glasses. Then he raised his eyebrows and turned to Audrey.

"I need to run more tests," he replied. "I also need to have someone look at the larvae we found inside the deceased's brain. I believe Somerset's biology department could help us here. It would help to know exactly what we were dealing with."

Danny blinked, glanced over at Audrey, who looked at the M.E. "Wait a minute, Walter. Haven't we been over this? They're botfly maggots or whatever."

"Not quite," Dr. Slikowski replied.

"Confused," Danny announced.

The M.E. sighed. "The botfly's usual method of reproduction is to capture a mosquito mid-flight, and then deposit an egg on its proboscis. When the mosquito bites a cow or a person or what have you, it unwittingly implants that egg beneath the skin of its victim. The egg becomes a larval stage botfly under the skin, and a large pimplelike lump develops on the surface. When it becomes a fly, it simply leaves."

The doctor paused and glanced out the window for what seemed to Danny to be an awfully long time. It was clear that he was troubled. Which Danny took to be a bad sign. Nothing ruffled Walter Slikowski.

"But . . ." Audrey began.

"Yes," the M.E. agreed, cutting her off and pushing

back slightly in his wheelchair. "Somehow, our insect managed to get into Mr. Garson's brain. Perhaps through the ear canal, originally. There, it laid dozens, maybe hundreds of eggs. All of the information I've been able to find would indicate that this is not only unlikely, but impossible on several levels.

"Unless this is something other than a botfly. Something there isn't any research on yet."

They stared at him. Dr. Slikowski swallowed.

"Something that's carrying an incurable, fatal disease."

Danny let out a long breath. "Oh boy."

Later that night, Jenna was in a crowd again. This time it was inside the arts house, a three-story residence that had been converted into specialized housing for students with an interest in the arts. The entire structure shook with music from Madonna and Culture Club and Tears for Fears and other eighties flashbacks. That was the theme of the party, actually, and Jenna was loving every minute of it.

Dressed in black jeans, black Steve Madden platforms, and a black baby tee with spaghetti straps, Jenna felt about as daring as she ever got. But she also felt good. Yoshiko and Hunter had moved off into the crowd, likely in search of punch, leaving Jenna and Melody dancing like wild girls, sweating profusely even though every window in the place was open, but not caring a bit. She'd spent half an hour fixing her hair, and now it was flatter and stringier than Alanis Morrissette's worst nightmare.

Jenna didn't care.

The place was rocking.

"I love this!" she cried to Melody, straining to be heard over the music.

Melody only nodded at first. Then she danced a little closer, blond curls whirling around her shoulders, and shouted, "I only went to one frat party my first year. I think everybody has to go to one. This kind is way better!"

Jenna raised her eyebrows. "Why?"

"The guys here are cool. The straight ones don't just assume that you're going to sleep with them because you dance with them. Plus the lingering odor of beer vomit at frat parties kind of curbs the fun quotient."

With a loud laugh, Jenna whipped around, spinning to the music, and then pulled Melody into a hug; just before she gave her a playful shove.

"You're something else, LaChance!" Jenna said loudly.

Madonna sang the last few notes of "Borderline" and the two girls paused in their dancing for a moment. Melody was grinning, sweating, just like Jenna.

"Yeah," the sophomore agreed. "I am, aren't I?"

The music flowed. So did the drinks. Melody gossiped about professors, and Jenna loved it. She also revealed more about herself and her brother than Jenna had previously known. They came from old Louisiana money, and their father had died several years earlier, after their mother divorced him for "running around." Before he died, Mr. LaChance had lived in New Orleans—which Melody pronounced N'Awlins—while Mrs. LaChance lived a ways up the Mississippi in a sprawling country house that her children missed terribly.

"Wouldn't trade it for her, of course," Melody added. "But it's a perfect place to go home to."

Jenna had pictures of Scarlett O'Hara in her head when Melody added, "And of course y'all know my little brother's got a mad crush on you."

Jenna blinked. "Huh?"

Melody smiled. "Don't tell him I told you."

"Don't *you* tell him you told *me*." Jenna glanced around. "I think Yoshiko likes Hunter, and I don't want him getting any ideas about me and him."

"You got it," Melody said, and then reached out to take Jenna's hands as the music picked up speed.

They spun around until the song was over.

Then something slow began, another forgotten eighties song by Richard Marx. Jenna was still laughing and was about to say something to Melody when a warm body stepped between them. A warm, very handsome body.

"Hey, Jenna," Damon Harris said, with a smile that melted her where she stood.

"Hi," she replied, because she couldn't think of anything else.

"Want to dance?"

Butterflies flitted around her stomach and she looked around for Melody, who only grinned and nodded, urging her on.

"Sure," she said uncertainly, taking Damon's hand.

So they danced.

And it went great.

Until she mentioned she'd just gotten a job, and Damon asked her what it was . . . and she told him.

He looked at her a bit oddly, but it passed, and they kept dancing until the end of that song. And then he said he needed to run upstairs to the bathroom.

Damon didn't come back.

A little while later, she bumped into Melody in line for drinks.

"What happened to tall, dark, and wow?" the other girl asked.

Jenna shrugged, rolling her eyes heavenward. "We were talking about my new job." She could hear the tension and disappointment in her own voice, but there wasn't anything she could do about it. "Now he thinks I'm freaky chick or something."

Melody smiled and shook her head. "You don't know that," she said. "Maybe he ran into some friends, got talking to someone else. That's what happens at a party like this, right? Don't go all paranoid on me, all right? He lives on your floor. You'll see him again."

Jenna offered a halfhearted smile. Melody bent over, eyes wide, glaring at her.

"So it's a little freaky," she said. "He's a smart guy. He'll get over it. And if not . . . you have a whole campus to choose from. You've only been here three days, darlin'."

"Right," Jenna agreed, nodding. "What's my rush?"

"My question exactly," Melody replied enthusiastically.

They exchanged a look that said they both knew she still felt bad about being ditched, but Melody wasn't about to let it get her down, and Jenna silently promised to get on with the business of having fun.

Which was when Michael Jackson came on the CD player singing "Billie Jean."

Melody cringed. "Y'know," she said, "there's a limit to how much eighties music anyone should listen to in one stretch."

"I'm with you," Jenna replied. "There oughta be a Surgeon General's warning or something."

But, though they longed for some real music, they kept dancing. Neither one of them was ready to quit just yet.

The rest of the weekend went by even more quickly, wandering around campus, hanging out at the campus center and the dining halls, trying to decide whether or not to audition for *The Sound of Music* . . . Jenna met a lot of people. Most of whom she knew she would forget almost immediately if she didn't see them again sometime soon. She made a mental note, on Sunday morning, to tell Melody that "the lingering odor of beer vomit" wasn't confined to frat houses, or even to the guys' end of the hall. Jenna hoped she never humiliated herself like that. Especially not in front of anyone she knew. At least two of the girls on her floor had already shown themselves not to have the same concerns.

On Monday morning, she had a revolting omelette for breakfast. Though she had plenty of money saved up from her various jobs in high school, and from family gifts, she didn't want to spend it *all* on takeout. At least, not just in first semester.

Her Fundamentals of Biology class started at 8:50, which was too early by far. *What a way to start my college career.* But after the basic introductions, the class turned out to be pretty interesting. Over the summer, the professor had been doing research into the mystery behind the fact that sharks do not get cancer.

Later in the morning, she had her first Spanish class. The teacher was mildly annoying, in that she treated most of her students as though they were kindergarteners. But Jenna had had teachers like that more than once in high school, and so merely rolled her eyes from time to time.

She ate a quick lunch at Nadel Dining Hall, down the hill, chatting with a girl she'd met in her Spanish class. Then, at 12:50, it was time for the class she'd been most looking forward to. There were so many required classes in the core curriculum that she was automatically more interested in her electives, the classes she got to choose just because they sounded cool. International Relations was one of those. With each semester, she'd need to concentrate more and more on her eventual major, so she wanted to be as diverse as possible before it was too late.

It didn't hurt that the professor was her father's good friend, José Mattei. I.R. was held in Ballard Hall, up on the academic quad, in a tile-floored classroom that had seen better days. But the building itself was beautiful, with enormous, many-paned windows that seemed to stretch nearly from floor to ceiling, and woodwork that seemed out of place in a classroom.

The room was also drafty, and it was a chilly day for September. Jenna kept her jacket on as she sat with forty or so other students, all waiting for Professor Mattei.

And waiting.

By the time he arrived, it was ten past one, and several students had already left, assuming the professor wasn't coming. Jenna had thought briefly about leaving, but didn't want to make a bad impression if he was merely late. Which he was.

But when he did show up, she stopped worrying about bad impressions. Professor Mattei was a mess. His clothes were rumpled and his hair was wild, as though he'd slept on it wrong and hadn't bothered to comb it in the morning. His eyes were bloodshot and his expression angry. His jaw was set as though he were grinding his teeth, like he was furious about something or other. It might have been just that he was so late, and angry at himself, but Jenna didn't dare ask him. In here, she was just a student, not the daughter of a good friend and colleague.

The desks were lined up seven by seven, in front of a broad wooden desk and chair for the professor. He ignored that. Instead, he went to a podium at the head of the class, just in front of the blackboard. Then he turned, and started to write on the board.

He hadn't said a word.

At the desk next to Jenna, a tall Asian guy muttered,

"This semester's going to be a joy," with as much sarcasm as she'd ever heard in anyone's voice.

Professor Mattei froze. He seemed to quiver a moment, and then the chalk in his hand snapped. Slowly, he turned.

"You," he said, glaring at the guy next to Jenna. "You've got something to say?"

His accent seemed thicker to Jenna, and she had no idea how he could have pinpointed the exact spot where the voice had come from. But he just glared at the guy, waiting for an answer.

"Not at all, Professor. I . . . I just realized I left my notebook at the dining hall," the guy said, thinking quick.

"Well," Professor Mattei said, drawing it out as he stroked his thin goatee. Then he smiled. "All right. But hurry back, all right?"

"Yes, sir," the kid said, but he wasn't in half as much of a hurry now that the professor seemed to have relaxed. He headed for the door.

Jenna let out a sigh of relief. Rather than being disturbed, as she had been moments earlier, now she was only concerned for the professor. His manner was so different today, she assumed that something awful must have happened to him. She'd have to ask her father later.

As the guy passed the podium and went toward the door, Jenna glanced out the window. The trees were still green, but it wouldn't be long, she knew. *It'll be a beautiful view when they start to change—*

A sudden clamor arose, and someone began to

shout. To roar. She spun around in her seat to see Professor Mattei grab the student on his way out the door, drag him back in, and begin pounding his head against the podium.

"There's no talking in class!" the professor shrieked, his voice thick and wild.

A couple of guys in the first row jumped up and tried to grab the professor. He backhanded one of them hard across the face and then kicked the other between the legs.

Someone was screaming. Jenna realized it was her. And she wasn't alone.

Then Professor Mattei did something unthinkable. He grabbed the Asian guy who'd decided to make a wisecrack in class by the hair and by his belt, and propelled him—the guy's feet stumbling along, trying to keep himself from falling—toward the window.

Right near Jenna.

She saw what was about to happen. It was insane. Impossible. But she knew it was coming.

"Professor, no!" she shrieked, coming to her feet just as several other students also rushed toward the thin, bespectacled man who was suddenly so very strong.

"José!" she screamed, hoping his name would bring him back to earth, back to reality.

He slammed the poor kid through the glass, the window shattering in sun-glittering shards. The kid's arms and face were cut, and his right leg snagged on a jagged chunk of window that stabbed up from the frame, before tearing free.

Then the kid fell, screaming, from the third story.

"Oh my God!" Jenna wailed. "What did you do? What did you—"

Professor Mattei spun on her. In that split second, she knew he was going to hit her. But she reacted too late, and his knuckles cracked across her cheek with great force, sending her stumbling back and to the floor.

Three students grabbed the professor and started grappling with him. More were moving in when she saw the blood begin to drip from his eyes. She stared at him, and saw that his ears were bleeding too. A tiny stream of it started trickling from the professor's nose, and a chill ran through her as she thought she saw something move there, just inside his left nostril.

"Get away from him!" she screeched, climbing to her feet. She grabbed at the other students. "Get away, you don't understand! He's got something, some kind of virus or something!"

Then the professor's entire body began to spasm, and suddenly, they could all hear her perfectly well. The students moved away from him as Professor Mattei collapsed on the floor in the midst of a fit of convulsions. His mouth was open and blood spilled out.

"Stay back!" she snapped, as one well-intentioned girl went to help the man.

The man. Her father's good friend. Who had told her to call him José.

He died right there at her feet.

chapter 6

Jenna was numb as she walked across campus toward her father's apartment. The sun had been blotted out by dark, heavy rain clouds which hung low overhead, and the temperature had dropped quite a bit. A shudder ran through her as she came in sight of the house he now shared only with Shayna Emerson.

For the resident of the top floor, her father's closest friend, was now dead.

Fat drops of rain began to fall and she shuddered again, but not because of the rain. Not because of the cold. She stopped across the street from her father's house and stared up at the windows, frozen in place. She said a silent prayer that someone—anyone—had called him already. That she would not have to be the one to bring him this news. It wasn't fair.

But she knew. And since she knew, she had to go to him, to tell him. There wasn't anything else she could do.

A bunch of guys swearing at each other and laughing rushed past her, maybe late for class, and Jenna was jostled a little bit. She barely felt it. Her eyes never left the second-floor windows of her father's apartment. Finally, with a deep sigh, she started across the street. A blue sedan paused at the intersection of Lewis and Sterling, and waited patiently for her to pass, though it seemed to her that it must have taken a million years.

She reached the opposite curb.

"Hey, Jenna!" a voice shouted pleasantly behind her.

She turned, unsmiling, and saw that it was Hunter, jogging across the street toward her. He had a wide grin on his face and a black canvas bag over his shoulder in which he carried his books and other things.

"What's goin' on with you?" he asked amiably. "I must have called your name five times."

Tears burned at the edges of her vision, but she would not let them fall. Instead, she took a deep breath, and then another, and she glanced up at Hunter with a look that wiped the smile right off his face.

"Whoa, Jenna, what'd I say? Did I . . . are you all right?" he asked, obviously confused and yet sympathetic. He was worried about her.

She shook her head. "Sorry, Hunter," she mumbled. "I can't . . . I've gotta talk to my dad, okay?"

He looked at her oddly a moment, then nodded urgently. "Yeah, okay. I'll be back at the dorm later, if you want to talk."

She forced a smile, but only for his benefit. "Thanks."

When he was gone, she took another breath and started up the stairs to her father's door. She pressed the buzzer for the second floor, and then she waited. After a few seconds, she tried again.

She almost walked away. Then: "Who is it?"

"Dad, it's me."

"Jenna?" His voice was filled with questions. Didn't she have class? Why the surprise visit? Why the quiver in her voice? "I'll be right down," was all he said.

The dead bolt was so loud as he unlocked it that Jenna jumped a bit, startled by the sound. Then he hauled the door open, and she looked at him in his rumpled clothes, with his graying beard and a small smile on his face. A smile that quickly faded.

She felt responsible, somehow, for the fading of that smile.

"I'm sorry, Daddy," she said, thinking that her voice sounded as though she were still a little girl. And that was how she felt. "I'm so sorry."

He reached out to her. "Come in out of the rain."

She melted into his embrace, hugged him so hard she was afraid she might hurt him. The tears began then, scorching her cheeks as she sobbed. As calm as she had tried to be, as much as she had tried to help, the horror of what she had seen only a short while earlier still lingered. It came back to her now in vivid, devastating images.

"What is it, Jenna? What's wrong?" her father asked, so kind, so worried for her.

Then she knew that she was being selfish. She had come here to comfort him, not to be comforted. After all, Professor Mattei had been his best friend.

Jenna pushed away from her father and angrily wiped the tears away from her face.

"Sorry," she said again.

"Stop saying that," he chided her. "Just tell me what's wrong."

"I just came from class," she began. She almost broke down again, but refused to allow herself to do so. She took a breath, and said, "Professor Mattei's class."

"And?" her father asked, eyes widening.

Jenna bit her lip, reached out and took her father's hands. "He's dead, Dad. José is dead."

Her father looked as though she had punched him in the gut. He stumbled back a couple of steps and sat down hard on the stairs in the foyer. Frank brought his hands up to his face and breathed deeply into them, staring off into nothing. Then he bit his lip, just like Jenna did, and tears began to well up in his eyes.

Frank reached out for his daughter's hands and pulled her to him. She sat down next to him on the steps and he hugged her, placing his chin on the top of her head. Holding her like that, he asked: "What happened?"

And she told him. About all of it. The truth about the autopsy she had witnessed on Friday, and the way Professor Mattei had died, and that he'd murdered a student, and that she had tried to help but just couldn't. Just couldn't.

"There wasn't anything you could have done, baby," he told her.

Jenna knew he was right, but something in her rebelled at the idea. *There should have been something I could do.* She was convinced of that. *There ought to have been something.*

"Is it spreading?" her father asked. "Some kind of virus?"

"Not according to Dr. Slikowski," she replied. "But . . . maybe you should call him."

"I guess I'd better," Frank replied. "I want to get to the bottom of this."

It wasn't long before a few phone calls turned up some disturbing facts. The school and the police had tentatively attributed Professor Mattei's death to a brain hemorrhage. Walter Slikowski knew what it was, but he assured Frank Logan that it wasn't contagious. Jenna wasn't going to get it, at least not by being in the room with a victim. No, the disease was contracted in some very specific ways, which he couldn't really discuss at the moment.

"It fits that he was from Costa Rica, though," Dr. Slikowski told Frank. "Had he been there recently?"

"Not in more than a month," Frank told him.

Which made Walter fall briefly silent. "I'll keep you posted," he said at last. "Tell Jenna she can put off starting work a few days."

★ ★ ★

When he was off the phone, Frank filled Jenna in on the conversation. She frowned at Slick's remarks about work. She was going, no question about that. If nothing else, that's what she could do for her father. Be a part of the effort to find out what killed his friend and colleague.

Later, she boiled pasta for dinner and they poured some sauce from a jar over it and it didn't matter that it wasn't very good. Neither of them could taste a thing. The shock was too fresh.

They sat and talked together for a while, until Jenna realized that her father probably had things he had to do, including talking to some of the other professors about it, and dealing with his class preparations for the next day.

"I should go," she said, pushing away from the table and carrying her ice cream dish to the sink.

"You don't have to," Frank said. "You could stay here if you want."

Jenna was tempted. But her father wasn't the only one who had things to do. She had a biology assignment to read, and an essay, which was basically "What I did this summer," for Spanish class. As much as she might like it to, school wasn't going to just stop because two people had died. Not unless it was an epidemic of some kind.

In the shadow of death, life goes on. She'd heard her mother say that several times over the years. Only now did she understand what it really meant.

* * *

Walking back into her dorm, Jenna felt almost invisible. She passed through little clutches of students in the lobby, on the stairs, and on her floor. Some said hello, and she mumbled a response. For the most part, however, she drifted among them, set apart from the other students by her proximity to the deaths she had witnessed that day.

She reached into the pocket of her jeans and fumbled with the plastic coil attached to her keys. As she put the key into the lock, the door was hauled open from the inside. Startled, Jenna looked up and blinked several times as Yoshiko reached for her hand.

"Oh, God, Jenna," her roommate said, face etched with concern. "I was so worried about you. Where were you?"

"I went to see my dad," she replied, and gave a small shrug. "Guess I should have called."

Yoshiko shook her head. "No, no. I was stupid. Of course you'd go to your father's. Your mom called a couple of times. She's pretty frantic, so you should give her a call."

Jenna did so. The conversation with her mother lasted less than ten minutes. She assured April there was nothing she could do. That she was fine. That she'd try to come home for dinner the following Saturday, though she really didn't think she'd end up doing so.

When there was a knock on the door, she told her mother she had to be going, and hung up.

Yoshiko opened the door and let Hunter in.

"Hey," he said uncomfortably.

"Hey," she replied, and shrugged helplessly. "Sorry I was such a zombie earlier. I just . . ."

"No, that's cool," Hunter replied. "I didn't know about it until two hours later. Then I realized you were in that class, and I put it all together. You okay?"

"Not really," she said honestly. "But I will be. If I don't dream tonight."

Hunter clearly didn't know what to say to that. Yoshiko was sitting on the edge of Jenna's bed, looking pretty pitiful herself, as far as Jenna was concerned.

"Can we just hang out?" Jenna asked. "Watch a movie or something?"

"Sure," Yoshiko said. "That's a great idea."

"I'll hit the video store if you want," Hunter offered. "What do you want to see?"

Jenna offered a wan smile. "Nothing bloody."

Hunter went out right away. Jenna could see that Yoshiko wanted to ask her more about what had happened, but didn't dare, and she was glad. She didn't want to talk about it anymore. A few minutes later, Melody called to check on her, and they talked briefly before Jenna promised to call her the next day.

By the time Hunter returned with a sappy Meg Ryan movie, Jenna was fast asleep. She woke several times, her eyes fluttering open to find Yoshiko and Hunter sitting together on the floor watching the movie with the sound turned way down.

She felt better just knowing they were there.

Jenna had no dreams that night.

*　　*　　*

On Tuesday, Jenna walked into the medical center without hesitation. She had slept well, and woken up determined to deal with the horror of the day before. Her classes that day—Europe to 1815 and Continuity of American Literature—had been interesting, and she had actually enjoyed them. She heard a lot of people speculating about Professor Mattei's death, and simply chose to keep her mouth shut. She and her father had agreed that was the best course of action, at least for now.

No need to start a panic without more information.

She had a quick lunch with Melody and Hunter—Yoshiko was still in class—and then went back to Sparrow Hall to change before going to the hospital. She wore loose brown pants and a green knit top that she thought was conservative enough. Boring colors. But what the hell—she was working in an autopsy room.

When she arrived, she went straight up to Dr. Slikowski's office, but he wasn't there. Neither was Dyson. Since she had no idea where they were—possibly out at lunch, at another hospital, meeting with police or forensics specialists somewhere—all she could do was sit down and wait.

For twenty minutes, she stared at the rather uninspired collection of art prints on the walls of the office. She took it upon herself to water a large spider plant that seemed kind of droopy and that she couldn't imagine either man laying claim to.

She watched the clock.

When it became too much for her, Jenna stood up, sighed, ran her fingers through her hair, and walked out of the office. She took the elevator all the way down. When the doors opened to the basement, she nearly bumped into an orderly as she was getting off. The chubby man looked at her suspiciously.

"Can I help you with something?" he asked. "You look painfully lost."

"I'm not lost," she said simply. "I work here."

"In the morgue?" the man asked, eyebrows rising. Then, as though someone had whispered the answer in his ear, he nodded slowly. "Oh, right. You're the new diener."

"No," Jenna said. "I'm a pathology assistant."

The orderly smiled. "Right, right. Sure. Enjoy your first day."

He stepped past her onto the elevator. Before the doors closed, Jenna turned and frowned at him.

"How'd you know it was my first day?" she asked.

The man grinned. "Because a diener *is* a pathology assistant. I'm Tony, by the way. Tony Xin."

"Jenna Blake," she replied, as the doors slid closed. "Nice to meet you."

Then she was alone.

The entire basement level was cold, as though the air-conditioning units keeping the morgue at a steady fifty degrees were working overtime, and the chill had seeped out into the rest of the floor. Thoughts of the morgue made her shiver. Dyson had shown it to her after her "interview," and the rows of metal drawers had seemed very ominous to her.

Maybe it was just that, to Jenna, a corpse was something to be noticed. A dead body was cause for some spectacle, or at least attention. But there, in the morgue, they were alone and forgotten. It was creepy. Just off the autopsy room, there was a separate "cold room," where they kept bodies if they took a break during an autopsy or were preparing for one, or whatever, but she knew that was just a holding area. Not the morgue itself. It didn't have that creep factor.

She didn't think she wanted to spend too much time in the morgue. Certainly not by herself. But she had to acknowledge that if she was really interested in doing this kind of thing for a living, she'd be spending a lot of time with the dead.

Which she could handle. *Which you can handle*, she told herself. She could handle death after the fact. That was doable. As long as she didn't have to actually be there to watch them die, as she had been yesterday, she'd be all right.

The morgue door was just down the hall. She passed right by it on her way to the autopsy room. When she opened the door, she came in on a full house.

Dr. Slikowski sat in his wheelchair examining Professor Mattei's internal organs. Jenna's stomach flip-flopped a few times, but then settled down. She felt as though she might cry, but pushed the tears back. He was dead. There wasn't anything to be done about that. The only thing to do was figure out why he died, and Slick was the best there was at that, or so everybody seemed to think.

Albert Dyson was behind the table, assisting in the autopsy. His curly hair seemed even wilder than usual, and his olive skin a bit pallid. Nearer to Jenna, but also wearing masks over their noses and mouths, were a man and woman she had never seen. But there was something about the way they dressed, the way they turned to look her over, that marked them as cops. Particularly the dark-skinned woman. Her eyes were hard and cold.

Jenna's eyes drifted back to Professor Mattei's innards.

"Hello, Jenna," Dr. Dyson said.

Slick looked up and frowned at her. "Jenna," he said slowly. "I thought you weren't going to start today. Perhaps this isn't the best time."

She tore her eyes away from the dead man and looked at her new boss. Behind his wire-rim glasses, his usually distant eyes were soft with sympathy, the skin at their edges creased with lines of concern. Jenna wanted to be annoyed by this kindness, but she couldn't manage it. He was a good man, and she was touched by his concern.

"You asked me to start today, here I am," she said. "I have to learn. Professor Mattei was a friend of my father's, but I only met him a few times. If I'm going to be this close to death . . ."

She let her words trail off, trying to think of an idea to complete the sentence. She didn't need to. Slick just nodded as he looked at her for a long moment.

Then he said, "Get some gloves and a mask on. And Dyson, get her a lab coat, will you?"

Dyson looked surprised, as though he had expected

Dr. Slikowski to do something else entirely. But he complied. Jenna went around the autopsy table, ignoring the huge rack of formaldehyde-preserved autopsy specimens—basically little chunks of human bodies—that lined a rack of shelves to one side. She went through a couple of drawers, filled with surgical instruments and heavy string she assumed was used to sew the corspes up when the autopsy was finished, before she found the mask and gloves she would need.

It would take time to get used to this place. To everything about it, in fact.

As she slipped on the lab coat that Dyson handed her, Slick glanced up at their silent guests and said, "Audrey, Danny, this is Jenna Blake. She's my new path assistant. Jenna, I'd like to you meet Somerset Detectives Gaines and Mariano."

At the mention of her name, Jenna noticed Detective Gaines stiffen slightly. She looked at the detectives.

"You're Frank Logan's daughter," the woman said.

"That's me," Jenna agreed.

Detective Mariano, whom Jenna couldn't help but notice had very nice eyes, tilted his head thoughtfully.

"You were there when this man died," he said wonderingly.

"That's right."

They both stared at her a long moment. Finally, Detective Gaines said, "We're going to want to ask you a few questions later."

Jenna agreed, and they left it at that.

Slick turned to her as she tied on the mask. "Are you sure you're up to this?" he asked quietly.

"Nope. But I'm here. I want to be here."

"All right, then," the M.E. said. "But if you change your mind, I won't hold it against you. This isn't a job for everyone, and this is a hideous way to start."

"It's all uphill from here, then, right?" she asked.

He didn't respond to that. Instead, he said, "Why don't you help Dr. Dyson weigh the organs."

Which was how Jenna ended up holding her late professor's lungs in her hands.

Afterward, she washed up in the sink in the autopsy room, and then went to the bathroom to wash her hands again. She tried desperately to get the smell of formaldehyde out of her nose, but it just wouldn't go away. She wondered if it would last forever, but that was ridiculous. Dyson had told her that over time, it became so familiar that you just didn't smell it anymore.

Jenna couldn't imagine it, but she figured it must be true. Her eyes and her nostrils burned whenever she went into the autopsy room, but the doctors didn't seem to be bothered at all. They built up a kind of resistance to it; got used to it in the same way they must have gotten used to spending their days cutting up dead people and fishing around their insides for the clues to the mystery of death.

She wasn't sure she ever wanted to get used to any of it. But she supposed it was better than the numb feeling that she had now.

When she walked out of the bathroom, Slick and Dyson were talking to the two detectives in the corridor. Mariano—Danny, Slick had called him—turned to look at her, and offered a warm smile. Jenna blinked, and found herself smiling back. He must have been easily thirty years old, but he was a very handsome guy. And those eyes.

Just what she needed right now, a distraction.

She laughed silently at herself, and was glad to know that, after the past twenty-four hours, she could laugh at all.

Dr. Slikowski acknowledged her with a slight nod, but went on with his conversation with the detectives.

"So it's definitely the same thing, but you're sure it isn't airborne?" Detective Gaines was saying.

Jenna thought that her jaw was a bit clenched, and wondered if the woman was always that tense.

"CDC is sending someone up this week," Dyson began, but Slick cut him off with a look.

"It isn't airborne," the M.E. said.

Dr. Slikowski was in a wheelchair, which automatically put him at a disadvantage in a conversation with a group of people who were standing. But he was still the M.E. here. It was his show. That look was all Dyson needed to remind him who was in charge. Jenna admired that about Dr. Slikowski. He was pretty conservative: more like a grumpy Mr. Rogers than any of the doctors on television. But he was a man who commanded respect.

"CDC's going to grow a culture from the tissue sample we sent, but it's clear from the tests we did that both men had begun to develop antibodies, and the antibodies revealed something of the nature of transmission. Yes, the hemorrhaging resembles ebola in a way, but the disease is actually much closer to mad cow in nature," Slick explained.

"At this point, I think we need to contact an entomologist and see if we can track down exactly what kind of insect we're dealing with here. Whatever it is, the first thing to do is get it under control and keep it out of this country."

Detective Gaines was nodding. "We have someone on that. We're in touch with the congressman's office, checking to see where exactly in Costa Rica Garson had been while he was over there. Seeing if we can't find a commonality between his itinerary and Professor Mattei's."

Jenna frowned. Something didn't make sense to her.

"Professor Mattei was there more than a month ago," she said. "How could something like this take so long to develop?"

"That's one of the things we have to find out," Detective Mariano said.

Jenna looked at him, studied his face a moment. She was surprised that none of them found this as odd as she did. Maybe it was because there were so many other unknowns here: trying to get CDC to identify the disease, finding a bug researcher to figure out what insect it was, tying it all to a location in Costa Rica.

But it made no sense to her.

The two men died the same way. If it incubated in

Nicholas Garson in a matter of days, it wasn't logical to think it could take a month to do so in Professor Mattei.

She sighed.

What do you know? she asked herself. *Leave it to the experts.*

And for a while, she forgot about it. She worked with the doctors the rest of the day, after the police had left, cataloging the results of the professor's autopsy.

When she left, Slick actually smiled. "You did well today. I don't know if I would have made it through that, if I were you. You should be proud."

Jenna was slightly embarrassed by his praise, but glad of it just the same. Dyson also complimented her, but his was limited to "Way to go, kid."

But on the walk home, her mind returned once again to the thing that had been bothering her earlier. The timing of Garson and Mattei's deaths simply didn't make sense.

No sense at all.

chapter 7

On Wednesday morning, Jenna woke to find that the weather—which had been fairly nice since she'd arrived the week before—had shifted dramatically. Dark, heavy clouds blocked out the sky, and only a gray light filtered through the windows. The rain fell in a cold, steady spatter, and when the wind blew, it hit the glass with a sound like a hundred steel needles striking at once.

It was an ugly day.

Jenna pulled the covers up to her neck and lay there in the gray dark with the hostile weather whipping about outside, and she felt as though she might cry. The adrenaline that had been coursing through her the past few days, keeping her focused and intense, had slipped away during the night. Perhaps, she thought, it had been sucked out of her by the dismal day.

More likely, she had just been suppressing her horror and despair. Now it all came tumbling down upon her in a wave. The autopsies, she could handle. She'd proven that to herself. It wasn't the job. It was that Professor Mattei had lost his mind before her eyes, had killed a boy whose name she still did not know, and had then died at her feet.

Most people—and now she recalled Damon Harris in particular, the guy who'd blown her off over the weekend after learning she was a path assistant—were put off by what she was doing for work. They couldn't understand how an eighteen-year-old-girl could stomach participating in an autopsy. Never mind the sexist crap involved in that idea, it wasn't much of a surprise. In truth, Jenna was surprised herself at how easily she had adapted to the concept. To being around death.

But witnessing death—being on hand for violence and murder and insanity—that wasn't part of the job.

A chill coursed through her that had nothing to do with the cold rain pounding the windows. She lay there, trying to get warm under her covers, thinking about how she didn't have an umbrella, and how her 8:50 bio class, though only about a hundred yards from Sparrow Hall, still seemed far away this morning.

The door opened and Yoshiko came in, a towel wrapped around her hair and a thick cotton robe tied around her waist. When she saw Jenna lying there in bed, her eyes widened a little.

"Hey," she said. Still staring at Jenna, she unwrapped the towel and dried some of the excess moisture in her hair. "You feeling okay?" Yoshiko asked.

"I guess," Jenna replied.

" 'Cause, y'know, you have class in, what, twelve minutes?"

"I know."

Yoshiko shrugged. "Okay, just so you know."

She blow-dried her hair quickly, not bothering with any makeup—not that Yoshiko ever wore that much anyway—and dressed quickly. She went over to Jenna's bunk and sat on the edge to slip her socks and shoes on.

"It's all getting to you, huh? The job, I mean," Yoshiko said. "You don't have to do it, you know."

Jenna smiled thinly, shook her head. "It isn't the job," she said, marveling that the conversation so closely mirrored her own thoughts from minutes earlier. "I think I just need to spend the day in bed, watching bad television, maybe catch up with some old friends by e-mail. God, with this weather, I think you're the crazy one for going outside at all."

Yoshiko glanced out the window, then back at Jenna. She smiled.

"Maybe you're right," she said, and lifted up the covers. "Make room."

Jenna laughed as the other girl slipped into the narrow bed with her, fully clothed. "Your sneakers better be clean," she told her roommate.

Together they looked up at the metal mesh of the bottom of Yoshiko's bunk. Yoshiko had her arms behind her head as if they were staring up at the stars.

"You want to talk about it?" Yoshiko asked, without even glancing at her.

For a moment, Jenna said nothing. She thought

about changing the subject, maybe asking Yoshiko if Hunter had noticed her existence yet. But that wouldn't really be fair. Yoshiko was trying to help.

Without looking at her roommate, Jenna said, "I was really scared, y'know?"

"Who wouldn't be?" Yoshiko asked. "You'd have to be brain-dead not to be terrified, Jenna. The guy threw a kid out the third-story window."

"I've never been so scared."

Yoshiko sat up in the bed, legs crossed, and looked at Jenna with great sympathy.

"You're okay, though," Yoshiko reassured her. "It's all over, right?"

"Right," Jenna agreed.

"You don't sound convinced."

"I'm not. But I guess it'll keep, right? You're going to be late for class. You should get going."

Yoshiko smiled kindly, then rose from the bed and went to her closet, from which she retrieved a light slicker and an umbrella. She slipped the jacket on, grabbed her backpack, and then turned back to Jenna, who hadn't moved an inch, except to pull her covers up again, smoothing them down where Yoshiko had been.

"Enjoy the talk shows," Yoshiko said.

Jenna didn't respond at first. Then she made a face, sighed, and threw back the sheet and blanket. Yoshiko only looked at her, eyebrows slightly raised.

"It's the first week of classes," Jenna said. "I guess it isn't the time for me to start blowing off whole days of school. Not unless I want to fall terminally behind."

Yoshiko smiled, brushing her straight, short black

hair back from her face as she reached for the doorknob.

"Plus, I guess I'd better go and find out if I'm even going to have an International Relations class this semester, after, y'know . . ."

"Probably a good call," Yoshiko replied, as she pulled open the door. "So you'll be late for class. I'm sure the professor will understand."

"We'll see," Jenna said. Then, just before the door closed, she called out to Yoshiko. The other girl poked her head back into the room. "Thanks," Jenna said.

"What are roomies for?" Yoshiko asked.

Then she was gone.

Jenna showered and dressed as fast as she could, and, since the bio lab was only right across the quad, managed to get to class less than half an hour into it. Professor Lebo, an older woman with her gray hair pulled back in a severe braid, offered her a questioning glance. Jenna ignored it and took her seat.

But while she listened to the rest of the professor's lecture, she recalled something Dr. Slikowski had said after the autopsy of Nicholas Garson. It led her to wait around when the rest of the students filed out at the end of class. The professor was glancing through some notes at the front of the class when Jenna approached. The woman looked up, and recognized her immediately.

"Ah, yes, our latecomer," she said, though her manner was not nearly as severe as her appearance. "I'm afraid if you want to catch what you missed, you'll have to talk to one of the other students. I don't have notes that anyone could decipher."

Jenna hesitated a moment. She was just a student; a freshman in college, without any authority nor official capacity in regard to Slick's office. But she did work for him. And she was curious.

"Actually, I was hoping we could talk about something else," she said. "I was wondering if you'd spoken to Dr. Slikowski about the botflies yet?"

The professor frowned, looked at Jenna a bit more closely, and stood up straight.

"I'm sorry, Miss . . . ?"

"Blake. I'm Jenna Blake. I work for the M.E., and I was just curious about the case," she said.

Professor Lebo blinked several times.

"I see," she said, after a long pause. "I'm sorry if I seem surprised. It just seems so unusual for—"

Jenna rolled her eyes. "For a girl to be working in the pathology department. Yeah, everybody has that reaction."

"That's not what I was going to say, actually," the professor said. "I was going to remark about your age. You are a freshman, yes? I thought so. I was also going to ask why, if you're involved in this 'case,' as you called it, you wouldn't have any information you'd need from Dr. Slikowski."

The classroom had started to fill up with students preparing for the class that would follow, so Jenna and Professor Lebo began to walk together toward the door. Jenna was a bit annoyed by the woman's attitude. It wasn't as though the thing was some big secret. What difference did it make if they talked about it or not?

Unless Slick told her about the disease, Jenna thought suddenly. After which, the woman's standoffish behavior became much easier to understand.

"I know everything that they knew, as of yesterday," Jenna said. "I haven't gone in today, and I'm kind of curious about all this myself. I just thought, if he hadn't called you, I'd save him the trouble."

Outside the classroom, the woman looked at her a moment. Then Professor Lebo seemed to relax a bit.

"Actually, I haven't talked to Dr. Slikowski in person," she admitted. "I spoke briefly to another man in his office, a doctor . . ."

"Dyson?"

"Yes, exactly. But Dr. Slikowski and I haven't connected yet."

It turned out that Dyson had told the professor about a possible disease carried by botflies, and how the botflies might be involved, and left it to Dr. Slikowski to have a more detailed conversation on that subject.

"Okay," Jenna said. "Here's the problem. I know botflies are supposed to breed by capturing a mosquito, putting an egg on the bug's stinger—"

"Proboscis."

"Right. Then when the mosquito bites someone, it plants the egg without even knowing it and a new botfly grows in there. But that's just one. Not, like, a whole city of them. So what's up with this?"

The professor walked beside Jenna to the door of

the lab. Outside, it was still raining, so they remained within the building's foyer as they spoke.

"There's a simple answer for that, but there's also a complex one. Which do you want?"

She wanted to say the complex answer, but Jenna was smart enough to know what she *didn't* know.

"How about a simple answer for starters," she replied.

"It isn't a botfly," Professor Lebo said.

Then she smiled, and waited for Jenna's response. One she was obviously expecting.

"So what is it?"

"I don't know," the professor said. "I'm going to be looking at some of the larval samples the docs saved for me. And I'm a biologist, not an entomologist, so they'll probably want me to get in touch with a bug person that I know. But I'll be able to provide more of a response when I've seen the samples.

"For now, though, think about it this way. The rain forests of Central and South America are believed to house many species of plant that have yet to be properly cataloged, and that is probably true of animals as well. Including insects. This thing may well be a relative of the botfly, but it isn't a botfly."

Jenna didn't have much to say about that. Until the professor could hook Slick up with an entomologist, or take a look at the larvae herself, they wouldn't know any more.

"Okay," Jenna said, nodding thoughtfully. "Thanks, then. I'll see you on Friday."

"At eight-fifty," Professor Lebo added, with a raised eyebrow.

The professor smiled, and together, they went to the door. The woman began to put her umbrella up, and Jenna pulled her jacket over the top of her head.

"I'll tell you one thing, though," Professor Lebo said.

"What's that?"

"I've never seen an insect crawl into the ear canal like that, and lay eggs in the brain. Disgusting. I'd be willing to chalk it up to coincidence, if it hadn't been for Professor Mattei. All I can say is, I hope there aren't any more of them around."

"No kidding," Jenna agreed.

Then they were out the door and heading their separate ways. As she ran back to her dorm, Jenna was extra careful about watching for insects.

Professor Mattei's International Relations class was canceled for the rest of the week, but a note had directed them to another classroom. There, a grad student from the I.R. department nervously informed the students that the faculty were presently trying to decide who was going to take over each of Mattei's classes, so they were to return to class beginning on Monday.

That took about ten minutes, after which Jenna had the day free. She didn't have to work that afternoon. In fact, she wasn't scheduled to go back in until Friday. She was glad of that. A couple of days without smelling formaldehyde would be quite welcome. Not to mention a couple of days without seeing any more dead bodies. She had grand plans—to hit the library and research Melville for her American Lit. essay, to explore Harvard Square, to check out Jah Man, a reggae club in Cambridge that Melody loved. *Yup, grand plans.* Most of which she already knew she wouldn't have the motivation to complete.

But she could try.

That night, she went to the movies with Melody and Hunter. Yoshiko was at a meeting for the school's literary magazine. She hoped to get on staff, or at least have something published by them. It was the first Jenna had heard of her secret passion for prose and poetry, and she resolved to spend some more time with Yoshiko.

In the meantime, she and Melody dragged Hunter to what he loudly complained was a "chick flick," which he ended up enjoying quite thoroughly, and the "chicks" themselves despised. Which, as far as Jenna was concerned, showed how in tune Hollywood was with her generation.

It wasn't until Thursday, after dinner downhill at Nadel D.H., that she got around to catching up with her old friends via e-mail. With distance between them now, it seemed like Moira and Priya had finally patched up their friendship. Jenna was happy, but not too surprised. If college was as hectic and exciting for them as it was for her—or even close—she figured their struggle over the affections of Noah Levine was just a bad memory.

Interestingly, though, she also got e-mail from Noah, who noted casually that he was back in touch with Priya. Which could possibly make the whole thing ugly again.

But there was something else in Noah's e-mail. The girls were much farther away, but Noah was at Umass, only a couple of hours' ride away. A fast trip. And gossip traveled even faster.

Dude, it began. Noah called everyone dude, though she didn't think he'd ever been surfing in his life.

> Dude, what a trip! What is going on over there? I heard some professor totally flipped it, killed some guy in the middle of class. Is it me, or didn't that kind of punishment go out a while back?
>
> So, what else is up?

The e-mail went on, and ended with the revelation about Priya. When Jenna went to respond, however, she was stuck on how to reply, exactly, to his comment about Professor Mattei's rampage. Eventually, she chose to ignore it, rather than have to explain the circumstances. But it was sort of eerie to realize that events there at Somerset had already rippled outward, touching other campuses, other parts of her life.

When she was through responding to her e-mail and creating a few new messages to Timmy Hargitay and several other friends who hadn't already contacted her, she decided to surf the Net for a while. Fiddling with her brainteaser puzzles, she searched for more information about botflies and other rain forest insects.

From there, she read a few articles about the Centers for Disease Control in Atlanta. Some of the viruses and the diseases the CDC had fought in the past few years terrified her. Some of them were airborne, and with the way people were packed in together on a college campus, and the behavior that usually went along with that . . . Jenna didn't even want to think about what would happen if one of those so-called supergerms ever got loose at Somerset.

There was a link to an article about biological and chemical warfare, and that gave her a chill as well. Knowing what the little "bugs" could do, she couldn't understand why anybody would *want* to let one loose.

Instead, she went back to reading about the rain forest, and about Central America in general, and Costa Rica in particular. She found it to be pretty fascinating stuff, and so, when there was a knock on the door just before seven, she was still entranced in her surfing.

"Just a second!" she called out, and broke the connection, freeing her phone back up.

When she opened the door, Melody was standing with her hands on her hips, exaggeratedly tapping one foot.

"Okay, so you're not dead," Melody observed, her sarcasm obvious. "I've been trying to call you for half an hour."

"I was on-line," Jenna explained. "What's up?"

"Hunter and I are going to auditions for *The Sound of Music*. I thought you might change your mind about trying out. Or at least come along for moral support."

Jenna frowned. "You don't need moral support for anything, Mel," she said. "You're about the most confident person I know."

Melody grinned. "You've never seen me onstage."

The two girls smiled at one another a moment, and then Jenna shook her head with a deep sigh. "I'll put my coat on," she said. "But no way am I trying out."

For the next two hours, she sat in the front row of Coleman Auditorium and watched a steady stream of moderately talented college students do their best to impress the two seniors who were producing and directing the show. Some of the potential cast members were truly awful. A few were wonderful. Hunter was one of those.

Melody, on the other hand . . . Melody was amazing.

Not that I'm surprised. I figure Melody does just about everything well. What did surprise her, however, was that she felt no sense of envy or jealousy about that fact. Melody was her friend, and that was that. It would have been very difficult not to like her, even if she wanted to try.

Sitting there, she was able to put thoughts of Professor Mattei's death out of her mind for the first time since she'd witnessed it. It was a nice feeling. Part of her wanted desperately to audition, or even to offer to help with the production in some other capacity, but she figured that with work, it would just be too much.

The more she thought about it, though, the more she started to talk herself into it.

If Melody gets cast, I'll try to get on the production staff, she decided. And she figured there wasn't a chance in hell that Melody wouldn't get a part. At the very least, the Baroness, or Liesl. Possibly even Maria.

Later, after Jenna had offered all the appropriate

praise, they were walking uphill toward Sparrow, and something funny occurred to Jenna.

"Oh, wow, you guys, I hope you remembered to tell them you were brother and sister," she said, a broad grin stretching her face. "It would suck if they cast you as Captain Von Trapp and Maria."

The twin looks of horror on the faces of her friends made Jenna laugh out loud.

On Friday afternoon, when Jenna arrived at work, Slick and Dyson were upstairs in the office. It was nice to have a slow day for once. They'd performed two autopsies that morning, and now it was just a matter of lab testing and paperwork.

"You'll learn to love paperwork," Dyson promised her.

"It's my life," she said.

"See, you've already got it down."

"Hey, paperwork's a joy. I mean, you can't be cutting up dead bodies all the time, right? So why not type up reports and transcribe sessions of doctors talking about cutting up dead bodies?"

Dyson chuckled. "Never thought I'd say this, Jenna. But I think you're going to do just fine here."

Later, while she was making some copies of a report for the police, Dr. Slikowski returned to the office, accompanied by two people she had never seen before. Pushing his wheelchair, something he tended to prefer doing himself, was a tall, lanky woman with bright red hair and freckles. Behind them came a broad-shouldered man with dark hair and a nose that looked as though it had been broken more than once.

"I suppose we'll simply have to be patient until the lab results are in," Slick was saying as they came into the office. Then he noticed Jenna and Dyson, and paused to offer them a weary smile before introducing them to the new arrivals.

"Ah, Dr. Martin, Agent Jeffries, I'd like you to meet my associates, Dr. Albert Dyson and Miss Jenna Blake," the M.E. said, then reversed the introductions. "Dr. Pamela Martin of the CDC, and Agent Arthur Jeffries, FBI."

They spent a few moments chatting amiably before Slick went into his office with Martin and Jeffries. Jenna watched them go in, then tried to go back to her work. But Slick hadn't closed the door, and she could hear their conversation fairly well.

"I think it's safe to say it's not a natural strain of anything," Dr. Martin was saying. "We should know a lot more once the results are back, but this thing has been engineered by somebody."

"How did the insects get it, though?" Agent Jeffries asked.

"There's no way to tell at this point if it's accidental or intentional. We'll just have to wait and see," Martin replied. "I'll keep you both posted. Agent Jeffries, can I reach you through the local authorities?"

"I'm coordinating with the local detectives involved with the case," Jeffries explained. "We're examining every possible angle."

Agent Jeffries left, and as he went, Jenna couldn't

help but compare him to Danny Mariano, the police detective she'd met earlier in the week. The two were polar opposites. Jeffries was cold and all professional. Danny just seemed warmer, more like someone who cared. If she was ever in trouble, she'd much rather count on Danny. Jeffries seemed like the type who might shoot through someone to hit his target.

You watch too much TV, Jenna told herself.

But seeing Jeffries had made her think of Detective Mariano. And that wasn't a bad thing. Not at all.

A short time later, Dr. Martin left as well. She barely acknowledged Jenna, or Dyson for that matter. *Two for two today,* Jenna thought. But at least Dyson and Slick were usually pleasant. Even if the job wasn't.

Just before quitting time, two victims of a car accident showed up at the hospital DOA on "the bus," which was what they called an ambulance. Dr. Slikowski was all for performing the autopsies that night, but Dyson convinced him the corpses would keep until the next day.

"They're not going anywhere, boss," Dyson said.

Slick gave in, and Dyson had the bodies brought to the morgue instead of the autopsy room.

Jenna was glad. She knew she was being oversensitive, but so many people thought her new job was ghoulish that it would be nice to be able to tell her friends that there were whole days she didn't have to watch corpses being cut apart. She hoped there would be more of them.

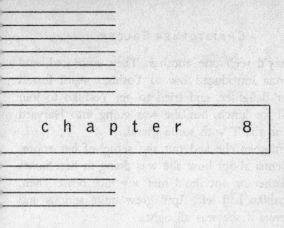

chapter 8

Jenna slept in on Saturday morning, and woke up with a smile on her face. The sun shone through the windows, and Yoshiko was sitting on the floor, doing leg-lifts and watching cartoons on television. Jenna stretched languidly in bed, and just lay there for a while watching *Dexter's Laboratory*.

"Morning," she said after a time.

Yoshiko looked up and smiled. "Slug."

"Guilty as charged," Jenna agreed.

Then, reluctantly, she crawled out of bed. It was nearly half past ten, and her mother would be there in another hour. They were going to go to lunch with Jenna's father, and then head into Boston for a shopping day.

Another reason for her to be smiling.

Life was good.

When April Blake arrived, Jenna was surprised at how much she had missed her mother in the week since they'd seen one another. They embraced, and then Jenna introduced her to Yoshiko. April fussed over her daughter, and tried to get Yoshiko to join them all for lunch, but she was going into Harvard Square on the T with some friends.

Her mother checked out the setup of her room, grilled Jenna about how she was doing in her classes and whether or not she'd met any nice boys. Then, after Yoshiko had left, April grew quite serious and asked Jenna if she was all right.

"I'm fine, Mom."

"No, I mean really."

"Really," Jenna insisted. "Okay, it was pretty upsetting, the whole thing with Professor Mattei, but the job is good. Really."

April grinned. "I'm so relieved," she said. "But you know what, I'm more proud than anything else."

"You don't mind that it isn't 'real' medicine? I know you wanted me to be a doctor."

"Jenna, just because it isn't what I do, doesn't mean I don't think pathology is real medicine. But you've got plenty of years to decide what you really want to end up doing. Besides, I want you to find something you feel passionate about, and make the most of it. I want you to be Jenna, not April," she insisted. "Hey, one of me is enough. I'm sure you'll agree."

"I plead the Fifth," Jenna said with a smirk.

Her mother raised her eyebrows. "Hey!"

"C'mon, let's go to lunch," Jenna said, rushing out the door.

Her mother pursued her, laughing. "Get back here, you fresh kid!"

A short time later, they were driving through Arlington, past the Capitol Theatre, with Jenna's father in the backseat. Her parents had been quite civil to one another, even pleasant, and Jenna wondered if it was just for her sake. On second thought, though, she realized it didn't matter why they were doing it.

Peace and quiet was peace and quiet.

They ate at a restaurant called Jimmy's Steer House, which turned out to serve far better food than a place called Jimmy's Steer House had any right to. There was venison on the menu, but no amount of prodding by her father could convince Jenna to eat it.

Cow was one thing. Pig another. Even lamb. But Bambi? *No freakin' way.*

About halfway through the meal, her mother paled slightly, then put her hand to her mouth. "Oh, Frank, I'm such an idiot," she said. "I wanted to tell you I was sorry about José when we picked you up, but we got to talking about everything else, and . . ."

"It's all right, April," Professor Logan said. "You called, remember?"

Jenna's mother nodded. "I'm sorry I couldn't make the funeral."

"You're a doctor," Frank replied. "You have responsibilities. I understand that."

They continued to talk, but now it was Jenna's turn to feel awkward. Not only had she not gone to Professor Mattei's funeral, she had purposely avoided it. She knew her father was going, of course. But she didn't like funerals, not at all. An autopsy, she could handle, the presence of a corpse, the medical investigation into death itself. None of that was a problem. But the result of death, the grief and the mourning of those left behind—and connecting her mental images from an autopsy to those of a loved one laid out at a wake—those were things Jenna couldn't bear.

"The administration has split up his classes among the present faculty, and asked Susan Cantor, who was on sabbatical, to come back a semester early," Frank said.

Jenna blinked. She'd been drifting, apparently, and her mother was wondering how the school was dealing with the death of such a popular professor.

"As for me, I'm handling some of his personal papers. José was working on a report on politics in Costa Rica that he'd wanted to submit to the papers, and such. I'm going to try to put that together as well," Frank explained.

"That's very gallant of you, Frank, but with your schedule, is it really wise?" April asked.

Jenna's father chuckled. "It's nice that you're concerned for me, April, but it's the least I can do; try to finish the work he started."

"Actually, I'm more concerned for Jenna," April replied.

Frank laughed, but Jenna looked at her mother in surprise. Here they had been behaving so sweetly to one another, and she has to say something so insulting. But Jenna's father didn't seem bothered by it at all. He looked amused if anything.

"What was he working on, Dad?" Jenna asked. More to change the conversation than anything else.

Frank smiled and leaned back in his wooden chair. The waitress came and refilled their water glasses, and April asked for more bread. There was music playing softly somewhere, and the restaurant lights seemed too dim compared to the sunlight streaming in the front windows.

"So curious," her father told her. "You've been that way since you were a baby. I think it'll serve you well as you grow older.

"As to what José was working on . . . well, you know he was Costa Rican. Though he'd lived here most of his life, he still had some family there, still kept track of doings all over Central America. Right now, they're gearing up for election season in Costa Rica. The front runner seems to be a man named Carlos Gutierrez.

"Gutierrez is a powerful speaker, a handsome man, and a favorite of the people. They love him."

"Why do I sense a 'but' coming here?" Jenna asked.

"But," her father replied, nodding, "there have been accusations that Gutierrez has connections to some of the largest drug cartels in South and Central America. Since Costa Rica has no military—"

"Really?" April asked. "None at all? That's amazing."

"Incredible," Frank agreed. "And in light of that, it's ripe for abuse by a corrupt government. So the opposition to Gutierrez is quite vocal, though very small at this point. Nobody has been able to prove a thing, and his handlers claim it's all a smear campaign. Which might very well be true."

Jenna frowned. "I don't get it. You mean nobody has been able to get the dirt on this guy? That just seems impossible. Unless there's no dirt to get."

"According to José's notes, a *Washington Post* reporter named Bernadette Knapp found a number of former associates of Gutierrez's who were willing to talk anonymously. She was apparently onto something, and then she died."

"What?" Jenna asked, staring at him. "How did she die?"

Her father looked puzzled. "I'm not sure. José's papers don't say. But he was starting to gather his own information, following as many of her contacts as he could. He never stopped caring about the country he was born in, and he wanted to keep Gutierrez out of power. If I can collect his papers, and organize his thoughts, and it gets into the right hands . . . well, I think that's a legacy he would appreciate."

"You're a good friend to do it," April told her ex-husband.

Jenna's eyes widened as she stared at them both. They started to chat about something else, and began to sip coffee the waitress had brought.

"Excuse me?" Jenna interrupted. "Could we get back to the bad guy for a second here? Some reporter gets near this Gutierrez guy's secrets, and she dies. Now Professor Mattei is dead, and so is a congressional aide who just got back from Costa Rica.

"Doesn't this strike you guys as odd?"

Both her parents, despite their years apart, gave her the very same look. A bit of love, and a lot of humor.

"Jenna," her mother said patiently, infuriatingly, "I know you're in college. I know you're excited, and this new job is . . . it's unusual at least, right? But when I was in college, I saw conspiracies everywhere. Ever since President Kennedy's assassination and then Watergate, it's all been about conspiracies. But this isn't alien invaders, and it isn't cold war espionage.

"Don't get carried away."

It took all Jenna's self-control not to storm out right then. "I am totally insulted by that attitude," she told her mother. "I'm not some psycho paranoid nutjob on the Internet, Mom. All right, maybe I'm jumping to conclusions, but you've got to admit, it's a little too convenient."

"Come on, Jenna," her father said, using a white cloth napkin to dab his mouth. "That aide had come back from Costa Rica. José was from there, and visited frequently enough."

"Not recently enough to allow for the incubation period of the bug in his head," she said bluntly.

Then instantly regretted it. Her father's face looked pinched, as her words reminded him of the horrible way his friend had died. She felt a bit guilty, but pushed the guilt away.

"You don't know that, because they haven't figured out exactly what the insect was yet," Frank told her. "I spoke to Walter Slikowski about it just yesterday. Worse-case scenario, according to him and the Centers for Disease Control, is that some insect life from the rain forest is foraging farther afield, and may start to infect more people in the near future. That's a scary thought. Horrifying, actually, given what this disease is capable of.

"But that's what it is, Jenna. A disease. Not political intrigue."

Jenna let the subject go after that. What her parents said, no matter how patronizingly they said it, made sense. But somehow, she just wasn't convinced.

On Sunday night, she spent a couple of hours with her nose stuck in *The Cougar Press Anthology of American Literature*, the fattest book she had ever owned. When she couldn't stand another moment of the scintillating prose of Nathaniel Hawthorne, she pulled on her coat and went over to Whitney House. Melody shared a room there with Angelina Brandolini, who was from Rome. There was a small clique of Italian students on campus, and Angelina spent most of her time with them. Which was fine with Melody. She and Angie had chosen to room together, but once they'd moved in together, they'd found they had little in common. Jenna sympathized. She was fortunate to have gotten Yoshiko, and by chance, too. Maybe they weren't going to be best of friends—she had bonded much more quickly with Melody—but they were definitely friends.

So they sat in Melody's surprisingly large double in the basement of Whitney House, eating pizza and watching an Emma Thompson movie about whiny rich people living in the English countryside. And loving every minute of it. At least for a while. When she got bored, though, Jenna began to tell Melody about her lunch with her parents the day before, and the questions that had been rolling around in her head.

"Just tell me one thing," she said, as Emma Thompson forced herself once again to keep her love for her brother-in-law to herself.

Melody couldn't tear her eyes away. Jenna could have told her how it was probably going to end. Namely: tragically. But she waited until the suspense of that particular moment was over before calling Melody's name.

"Huh?" Melody looked up.

"Just tell me one thing," she repeated. "Am I nuts? I mean, doesn't all this seem a little coincidental to you?"

"Well, I suppose," Melody said, and then shrugged. "But y'know, Jenna, I don't know how these imaginary bad guys would have known Professor Mattei was working on those papers to begin with. And how did they manage to get those bugs inside his skull? Never mind that disease."

"So I *am* nuts," Jenna said, kind of grumpily.

Melody peered at her more closely. "Hey, this is really bothering you," she said, as though she'd discovered something extraordinary. "Listen, you aren't crazy. But I think maybe you're looking at all of this too hard. Taking this job a little too seriously. Maybe after seeing what happened to the professor, you're just trying to make sense of it, y'know? Trying to find an answer that isn't there."

"Maybe," Jenna replied.

And yet, though she was more doubtful than ever about the things she had begun to suspect, she still could not shake the feeling that something sinister was going on.

Then she remembered that she hadn't asked Melody what had happened with the *Sound of Music* auditions.

"Weren't they supposed to post callbacks yesterday?" she asked.

Melody smiled.

"You made it!" Jenna cried happily. "That's great."

"It's only a callback. The real casting won't be decided until after the next round. That's on Tuesday night."

"Break a leg," Jenna told her.

On-screen, Emma Thompson had begun an affair with her sister's husband, and had been about to confess it, when her sister announced that she was dying of consumption.

Jenna rolled her eyes. She loved Emma Thompson movies. Particularly those about whiny rich people living in the English countryside. She only wished that, just once, everyone would live happily ever after, and all the people who deserved to get smacked in the head would get smacked in the head.

On Monday afternoon, a fiftysomething woman with close-cropped blond hair appeared before Jenna's International Relations class and introduced herself as Professor Gifune. She seemed pleasant enough to

Jenna, and her lecturing style was very instructive, but it was impossible to sit there and not remember the horror that had taken place the Monday before.

After class, she walked over to the medical center. Slick was in Boston, consulting on an autopsy at Mass General. Dyson hadn't had a day off for about two months, and it turned out today was the day. Which left Jenna by herself. Since she hadn't been at the job very long, that meant she spent the next few hours answering phones, taking notes, entering lab results into computer reports, and transcribing less than exciting autopsy narratives from the past couple of days.

She was amazed to find that, though she'd only been doing the job for a short time, she was already becoming jaded. Unless it was something absolutely ghoulish, or the death held some sort of mystery, there was very little to keep her captivated in Dr. Slikowski's droning descriptions of slicing up dead people.

Maybe this is the job for me after all, she thought. She didn't know anyone her age who would even want the job, never mind enjoy it.

By the time six o'clock rolled around, she knew she ought to quit for the day. She had promised Yoshiko they would hang out in the room later, and she needed to get some work done on her Melville essay and read a major bio assignment. Never mind the whole eating dinner thing.

But Dyson had been working too hard, and Slick was like the Energizer Bunny. Okay, in a wheelchair, but still, the man just never stopped going. If she took another hour or two, she could finish off all the reports and transcriptions that had piled up, and they'd have a clean slate in the morning.

"Yoshiko won't mind," she said aloud. *Ally McBeal* didn't come on until nine o'clock.

Jenna called Yoshiko, just to let her know she'd be a little later than she thought. Then she ordered a cheesesteak sub from Espresso's—one of the weaknesses that was sure to earn her the famed "freshman fifteen" pounds that most first-year college students seemed unable to avoid gaining.

Then it was back to work. But when she tried to think about work, her mind kept wandering. Back to thinking about bugs. About the disease, and the deaths, and the shady politician who wanted to be president of Costa Rica. And the reporter who died trying to find out more about him.

Jenna sat in front of the computer, desperately trying to remember the reporter's name. A woman's name. And a saint's name, if she remembered correctly. An uncommon one at that, not like St. Theresa or something. No, this was something else, a name like a man's.

Then she had it. Bernadette was the woman's name. Bernadette Knapp.

It only took her a few minutes to search the *Washington Post* database for the news story about Bernadette Knapp's untimely death. She was thirty-three when she died, no family except for her cats.

The paper said she died of a brain aneurysm. That was it. There were no other details about her death, nor any clue that the police found anything at all suspicious about it.

But that wasn't enough for Jenna. The paper also said she'd been taken to St. Luke's Hospital in Arlington, Virginia, and was pronounced dead on arrival. She tried to access patient information at St. Luke's and came up with nothing. Jenna chewed her lip for a minute, thinking about how much trouble she could get into for doing something like this.

"I've got to know," she whispered to herself.

Using Dr. Slikowski's name and credentials, and the address and phone number of the office, she e-mailed an official request for a copy of the autopsy report on Bernadette Knapp.

When she was done, she let out a long breath and sat back in her chair. She had to know. That was all there was to it. And now, she'd know soon enough.

Forcing her mind away from the subject it truly wanted to dwell upon, she buckled down and went back to work. And work. And work. Her cheesesteak showed up at quarter to seven. A little before eight, her eyes started to cross. She decided it was time to pack it in for the night. No more computer screens for her tonight. Better to hang with Yoshiko for a little while, then get up bright and early and deal with assignments and essays then.

The administrative wing of the hospital was quiet, if not dark. Very few phones were ringing. There was a blanket of darkness outside the windows in Slick's office. She heard a metal clanking sound that she knew was the cleaning crew's cart moving through the hallway. It was kind of spooky.

While Jenna was slipping her coat on, the phone rang, and she jumped, her heart pounding. It sounded incredibly loud in the silence of the office.

"Pathology," she answered.

"Who is this, please?"

The voice was female, cold and arrogant. Automatically, Jenna was on the defensive. She knew it wasn't professional, but she responded with the same attitude.

"Who's *this?*" she demanded.

"This is Dr. Martin of the CDC. Is the M.E. available?"

Jenna bit her lip. Dr. Martin might not be the warmest individual—the one time they'd met the woman had seemed a bit cold—but she had to be courteous and respectful. *At least it isn't that FBI guy, Jeffries,* she thought. She'd met the two of them together, and as unfriendly as Dr. Martin was, at least she wasn't as obnoxious as Jeffries.

"I'm sorry, he's out on a consult at the moment," she said. "May I take a message?"

"Just that I called," said Dr. Martin. "Be sure he gets it."

"I'll do that."

When she hung up, Jenna wanted to scream at the ice queen. But she wrote the note and left it in Slick's in-box. With a sigh, she picked up her bag and headed out the office door.

In the corridor, she looked around and realized that

the cleaning crew had moved on. They must have realized she was still working and decided to come back. Who knew what floor or office they were in now. It was pretty empty in the administrative wing at eight o'clock on a Monday night. Jenna picked up her pace as she walked toward the elevator banks.

Just as she rounded a corner, she heard a door close behind her with a click. She paused to glance back, but it was pretty dark now that the crew had been through, and she didn't see any of the doors open. There were lights on behind the doors of several offices, but that was all.

Jenna was about to turn then, and move to the elevators. But she felt it. Creeping up her back. It was a cold, familiar feeling. The feeling she had always gotten as a girl when she had woken up in the middle of the night to get a drink of water. Her mother would still be sleeping, and Jenna would go into the kitchen. The window above the sink would be black with the dark outside, and all she could see in it was the reflection of the stairs behind her, and the front door at the bottom, with its own little windows.

She would be afraid then. But she would say nothing, never daring to wake her mother, who would only tell her she was being silly. Instead, she had crawled back into her bed and told herself over and over that there was nobody out there, nobody watching.

That was the feeling, that someone was watching. That somebody's eyes were on her.

Jenna didn't hear any footsteps rapidly closing in on

her. She didn't hear any more noises, or doors closing, or heavy breathing. In fact, she felt a little silly about the whole thing. But she hurried to the elevator and she tapped her foot rapidly as she waited for it to come, and when she jumped in, she did so quickly and pressed the button several times, urging the doors to close before someone else could get on.

"Okay, Blake," she said aloud to herself, "time to cut down on that caffeine intake."

Or maybe it's just time to make a rule about working late when nobody else is in? she thought.

At the lobby level, she stepped off the elevator into the chaos of a hospital, and felt better immediately. It wasn't the ER, so it was much quieter than during the day. But there were still plenty of people around, so that was all right.

Chuckling at her own goofy paranoia, Jenna picked up her pace as she moved along the path that would wind past the medical center, and then the medical school itself, and then across the street to the undergraduate campus of Somerset.

Her mind began to wander, and she let it happen. To Yoshiko, and just relaxing tonight. To Melody. Jenna would have to call her tomorrow to say "break a leg" again.

And at that thought, Jenna's mind suddenly produced a melody of its own. A song she loved from the movie version of that play. In a low voice, quiet enough so that she wouldn't be terribly embarrassed if someone were to hear her, Jenna began to sing.

"Perhaps I had a wicked childhood.

"Perhaps I had a miserable youth . . ."

Out of the corner of her eye, in among the trees that lined the path, something moved. Someone moved. Jenna stopped, turned, and stared into the trees and frowned. A shiver ran through her, and her breathing speeded up a little.

Just when she was about to explain it away as a cat, or a squirrel, or something, it moved again. And Jenna could make out the shape of a man. Hidden in the trees, and in the dark, all she could see was the outline of broad shoulders, and a hooded sweatshirt pulled up tight to hide his face in the night.

For a moment, the man didn't move.

Then he did.

Jenna ran.

And the hooded man came after her.

c h a p t e r   9

Jenna Blake was still alive because she'd been willing
to risk looking stupid. Inside the medical center, she'd
had the feeling someone was watching her. It spooked
her completely. So that when she came outside, and
saw the figure lurking in the trees just off the concrete
path, she took off running. What would be the worst
thing that could happen? He wouldn't follow her at
all, and she'd look like a lunatic to anyone who happened to see her sprinting down the path.

No, actually. That wasn't the worst thing.

The worst thing was, she was right.

Jenna ran.

Her heart pounded in her chest, felt like it was
rising, as though it might prevent her from swallowing. The soles of her sneakers slapped concrete,
and her eyes were wide, soaking in all the light that
was available. Suddenly, the sound of her own breath,

whistling in and out of her mouth, seemed impossibly loud.

She couldn't even hear the racing steps of the man behind her. The dark figure chasing after her in the night.

Jenna's eyes roved across the path ahead, searching for help. For anyone. For a witness to what was happening to her, to what horrifying, impossible things might yet happen to her if her pursuer were to catch her. She glanced to her right; her eyes scanned the windows of the medical center as she ran past. Many were lit, but she saw no faces, no one looking down to the path, with its lampposts throwing circles of light. They were supposed to be circles of safety, those lights. But not tonight.

No one at the windows.

She left SMC behind, and then the main medical school building loomed up to her right. Most of its windows were dark. She saw no faces there, either. At the center of the building, large windows showed a well-lit stairwell that led from ground to roof. Several people were moving up and down those stairs.

Jenna was about to scream.

Her labored breathing was loud, and she could hear the slapping of her sneakers again, and suddenly she had to pause to think. *I don't hear him!* What if she screamed . . . and he was gone?

Her face flushed red; she began to slow the tiniest bit. Jenna glanced over her shoulder, just to make sure. And there he was, hood pulled down to shade his face, so that it looked as though there was no face there at all. He was close. Too close. Close enough to reach out, grab her hair, and pull her down, and . . .

Jenna screamed. Turned face front and bent into her sprint, tried to pick up speed, to elude him.

She wished he would talk. Say something. Threaten her, somehow. Then at least it would all seem more real. Now it just seemed like some kind of nightmare.

"No you don't, you little . . ." the man snarled, as if in answer to her thoughts, and his fingers brushed the back of her jacket.

Jenna screamed again. She jerked away from him, trying to elude those fingers. Her right foot caught on something—the edge of the grass, where concrete met lawn—and she tumbled forward onto the ground. The man cursed. He couldn't stop running, so he jumped over her instead. Jumped over her, and then onto her. With his right knee on her back, he pinned Jenna to the ground.

It was all happening so quickly.

He bent over. Whispered in her ear. "Just relax, girl," he growled. "With you out of the way, it'll all be taken care of."

With a shriek of anger and pain, Jenna threw her head back. Her skull cracked hard against her attacker's nose. He cried out in pain, and she felt a bit woozy from the impact herself. But she couldn't allow herself to slow down. His words were clear: he meant to kill her. For the moment, though, he was off balance. She had to take advantage of that. Jenna brought her right arm back, elbow cocked to a point, and gave him a hard shot to the head. Her attacker nearly fell off her back. Jenna bucked, turned beneath him. Her right leg snuck out from under his weight, and she brought it up in a haphazard kick.

Then he was rolling on the ground, coming up to face her beneath a thick tree. They were far from the nearest lamppost now, and he was in a swath of shadow. His face was hooded, his hands were gloved. All she could tell was that he had light skin. Then her attention was diverted by a sudden flash of metal in his hands.

He had a knife.

"Leave me alone!" she screamed frantically, backing up. "Just leave me . . ."

And that was it. She had turned, and was running again. Once again, he was pursuing her. Her back ached where he had pressed his knee into it, and her lip hurt where she had struck the ground when she fell. But that pain disappeared as adrenaline pumped through her.

"Just die already," the man said, his gravelly voice full of exasperation.

Jenna began to cry. She couldn't help it. She was growing tired and she didn't want to die.

Up ahead, she spotted the end of the path, and the cars that were going by on Carpenter Street. Beyond them, she saw the dormitories rising up from the Somerset campus. There would be plenty of students out and about. She was sure of that. If she could just reach the street, and if the traffic was right, she might just make it across.

But she wouldn't. She knew that now. *He's too close,*

too strong, too fast! She could hear his ragged breathing, even heavier than her own now, just behind her. Jenna screamed again. It wasn't going to help. In another few seconds, he'd get a real hold of her, and then . . .

"Hey! Get the hell away from her!"

The shout was loud and angry and unmistakably male. Jenna glanced over to her right. Two men and a woman, medical students she guessed, had come around the corner of the school building, seen her, and were even now running toward her. She veered in that direction, and poured on the speed.

"Oh god, ohgodohgod . . . help!" she managed to croak, breathing so hard she could barely manage that much.

The two men went right by her, running back the way she'd come. The woman opened her arms, and Jenna went into them, nearly collapsing, her heart thundering against her ribs.

"Hey, are you okay? Did he hurt you?" the woman asked.

As she sucked in air, trying to catch her breath, Jenna only managed to shake her head. She wheezed a bit, but she was in pretty good shape. After a few seconds, her breathing slowed, and she turned to see the two med students walking back toward her.

"Did you get a good look at him?" one of the men, a blond, asked her.

Jenna thought about it. "No," she gasped. "He had his hood up. Plus, to be honest, I was trying to get away from him, not closer."

The man nodded.

"He slipped through those trees at the end of the path, then down the hill," the other man said apologetically. "We'd never have caught him down there. And it seemed more important that you were all right, I guess."

"We should call the cops," the female student said.

"Yeah," the blond man agreed. "It's crazy, though. It's usually pretty safe around here. I don't think we had a single attack like that all last year."

"None that were reported," the woman told him, frowning. "College campuses all across the country have plenty of sex crimes that don't get reported."

Sex crimes? Jenna thought. Then she understood. This woman thought the guy wanted to rape her. Though she was still too terrified to think altogether rationally, Jenna dismissed that idea. She remembered what her attacker had said. With her out of the way, "it'll all be taken care of."

He had an agenda. And she had a growing, and horrifying, certainty that she knew just what that agenda was. Or part of it, at the very least.

"This is not good," she whispered to herself.

An hour and a half later, she sat in an uncomfortable plastic chair next to the desk of a campus police officer who'd had to ask her to spell her name three times before he got that it wasn't "Jen" or "Jenny" or "Jennifer." The cop's name, oddly enough, was Kryczinsky. Jenna thought that anyone who'd had to spell his own name as much as this particular officer probably had, ought to be a little more sensitive about unfamiliar names.

But whatever. He was competent enough when it came to taking her statement. He had given a quick report to the dispatcher, who radioed out to the other campus police, and the Somerset cops as well, that an attack had taken place. Jenna had only been able to recall that he was just under six feet, give or take a couple of inches, that he was broadly built, but not heavy, that he'd been wearing dark clothes—navy or black—including a hooded sweatshirt, and that he was either Caucasian or Latino. But somehow, even with that meager description, the police were out in force, trying to find her attacker.

I'm the victim, Jenna thought. *If I can see how ridiculously hopeless this is, why can't they?*

But she didn't speak her thoughts aloud. Maybe they'd get lucky. Surely it wasn't all that uncommon. Criminals, despite what television and books had taught Americans, were not a very intelligent lot. And that logic would work just fine if this guy had been just another two-bit mugger or rapist or even murderer.

But he wasn't. She was quite certain of that.

Still, she sat and gave Officer Kryczinksky a very complete report of her activities from the moment she left Dr. Slikowski's office, through the attack, and right up to the point she walked in the door to the campus police station. In fact, she told him that story several times, repeating different elements of it as he wrote it down.

A slow night, apparently.

Then, just as the officer began to file her statement and told her he'd get someone to take her back to her dorm, Jenna looked up to see a familiar face. It took her a moment to recall his name. Danny, that was it. Detective Danny Mariano. His eyes roved across the room, and stopped when they'd found her, as though she were what he'd been looking for.

She was.

"Jenna," he said, walking over. "I heard the all-points on the guy who attacked you. I was nearby, and when I heard your name, I thought I'd come by and check up on you."

Officer Kryczinksky gave them a dirty look, as though their chat were keeping him from his duties in some way. But the room was quiet, aside from their presence. Still, Detective Mariano glanced around, noted a white door, and urged Jenna in that direction.

"Let's talk over here," he said.

From the squeaky clean but rapidly aging squad room of the Somerset University Police Department, Danny led Jenna into what was apparently the campus cops' break room or something. There were a bunch of dilapidated vending machines against one wall, and a pair of unmatched tables surrounded by a bunch of wooden chairs. A door on the far side was stenciled with the letters LOC ER ROO.

"So, do you want to tell me what happened?" Detective Mariano asked kindly.

"I . . . you know what? Thanks for coming down,

but I just told this story three times. They're not going to catch this guy. He knew what he was doing."

Danny frowned. "What does that mean, exactly?"

Jenna sighed. She'd kind of figured this was how it was going to be.

"Look, Detective—"

"Danny."

She glanced up. *First name basis?* It seemed like a strange moment for him to decide to get chummy. He could just be trying to make her feel comfortable, Jenna knew. On the other hand, he had seemed very concerned for her when he'd first come in.

A homicide detective. Even if he was nearby when he heard the radio report, why would a homicide detective take an interest in a botched assault on a college campus?

"Danny, why are you here?" Jenna asked bluntly.

He blinked. "I told you. I heard your name, and I was nearby . . . You work for Dr. Slikowski, and my partner and I owe him a lot. And she knows your father. And . . ."

His words trailed off, and Jenna began to smile.

Danny smiled back, and it was a bit disarming. He was very handsome for a policeman, and very young for a detective. Too old for Jenna, for sure. But still . . . okay, he was a total honey. None of which mattered at the moment.

There was more going on here than just simple concern.

"You know, don't you?" she asked.

He blinked, opened his mouth, started to shake his head.

"No, don't even!" Jenna said quickly. "I know you know. There's something else going on here, isn't there? Here I was about to tell you why I was sure this guy wasn't just a casual stalker, or whatever. But you think the same thing. That's why you're here."

Detective Mariano nodded slowly, then shrugged. "You got me."

"Why?"

He grew uncomfortable with that. "Look, my partner doesn't see any of this. She thinks I'm just connecting the dots because it makes things more interesting. And Slick sure doesn't see any relationship, other than tragedy."

Jenna grinned.

"What?"

"You call him that too? Slick, I mean."

Danny grinned back, flushed a bit with embarrassment. "Forget I said that, please."

"I'll think about it," she replied.

There was a moment of silence then, and a nice energy between them. Then Jenna blinked a few times and glanced around the room. *What's wrong with me,* she wondered. This was neither the time nor the place . . . nor was Mr. Thirtysomething-homicide-cop "the guy."

"What gave you the idea he was after you specifically?" Danny asked.

So Jenna told him everything. Or almost everything. She left out the part about the request for the Washington reporter's autopsy report. That could get her in trouble with everyone from her father to Slick to the school administration to the cops themselves.

When she stopped talking, Danny made a face. "That's it?" he asked, obviously disappointed. "He didn't say anything more specific?"

"Sorry," Jenna snapped. "If I'd known there were extra points I'd have stuck around a little longer."

He sighed. "You know that's not what I meant."

Jenna nodded. She did know. But she was too frustrated to care. Here was a cop who also suspected something bad was going down. But nobody believed him, either. All of which meant absolutely nothing.

"He didn't say anything else," she told him again. "But I think he may have been in the hospital before I left. Snooping, or whatever."

Danny frowned at that. "You didn't see him, though?"

"No."

"Huh."

"What does 'huh' mean?"

He shrugged. "I shouldn't even be talking to you about this. Any of this. I don't know what I was thinking coming down here."

"Sure. You just wanted to make sure I was all right."

He raised his eyebrows, gave her a surprised glance, and then stood up from the table. *So apparently the idea that you might be looking out for me makes you uncomfortable,* she thought. And she smiled. It gave her a bit of an ego boost to think Danny might be attracted to her. Old as he was.

"Y'know what? Ignore me," the detective said. "I've always been a little too interested in conspiracy theories. Gets me in trouble every time. I guess there's a reason why my partner and the M.E. both think I should look at the facts instead of play hunches.

"I'm glad you're all right," he told her. "I'm sure I'll be seeing you around Dr. Slikowski's office. Do me a favor, and don't mention that I got all Mulder on you, all right?"

Then, before she could protest, he went to the door of the break room, opened it, and slipped out.

Jenna hopped up and went after him. "Wait!" she called. She opened the door, and called out to him again. He stopped halfway to the exit, and she hurried to catch up, grabbing her jacket from Officer Kryczinksky's desk as she passed.

"There's something else," she said, swallowing hard.

Danny narrowed his eyes and looked at her. She could tell by the look on his face that he was feeling foolish. She didn't blame him. Everyone from the M.E. to the CDC and all points in between thought this was nothing more than a particularly dangerous fluke. A new supergerm like this could be devastating. That the two known cases had taken place so close together was merely a coincidence, dictated by the connection both victims had to Costa Rica.

It was so easy to believe in coincidence.

"What is it?" Detective Mariano asked.

"You're not nuts," Jenna told him. "A couple of hours before I left, I . . . well, I e-mailed an official request for the autopsy report on a *Washington Post* reporter who died while she was investigating the background of a Costa Rican presidential candidate."

Danny shook his head and rolled his eyes. "Do you have any idea how paranoid that sounds? Now I know why Audrey never listens to me."

"How paranoid is it that two hours later, when I leave, I'm attacked by someone who seems pretty clear that I'm his intended target?" she demanded.

That seemed to give him pause for a moment. Then he shook his head again. "Jenna, you're talking about one computer with confidential documents talking to another computer with confidential documents, over what is probably a secure line . . ."

"No computer communication is ever completely secure," she said quickly.

"But two hours later? Come on. To get the information, track it to its source, travel to the hospital, stake you out, then follow you when you leave? I really think you're reaching here."

Now Jenna was mad. "Y'know what?" she demanded. "I don't think you think I'm reaching at all. I think you just don't want to look like an idiot in front of your partner if you turn out to be wrong."

With that, she stormed out the front door of the campus police station and began walking up the street toward Memorial Steps. She heard Danny push out the door behind her, but kept walking, even as he called after her.

When he put his hand on her shoulder, she spun around angrily.

"What?" she snapped. "You know, you came down here for a reason. You think there's something more to this and you're not sure what it is, but since I'm some eighteen-year-old college girl and my theories are a little far-fetched, you treat me like I'm stupid.

"Well, I'm not stupid, Detective Mariano. Somebody tried to kill me tonight, and I think we both have a pretty good idea of why. Maybe when I've got my throat cut, or maggots in my brain, you'll believe me then!"

She threw his hand off and started off again.

"Jenna, wait!" he called.

Something in his voice stopped her. She turned to look at him. His expression revealed his indecision.

"At least let me drive you back to your dorm," he suggested.

She was about to snap at him again, to turn and storm off, to walk home alone in spite of her fear. But she couldn't. He wanted to drive her because, no matter what he said, he did believe she might be in some danger.

In her mind, she could still remember the sound of that voice, gravelly and cold. "Just die already." That's what he'd said.

"All right," she told Danny.

She was glad of the ride, though they barely spoke, each alone with their own thoughts. When he dropped her off, she ran quickly to her dorm. When she came in, and locked the door, Yoshiko sat up on the top bunk and looked as though she were about to curse Jenna out. After all, Jenna was hours later than she'd said she would be. They'd had plans to hang out and watch *Ally*. Yoshiko had stayed in, waiting for her, worrying about her.

Jenna could see all of it on her face, in that angry glance.

But then Yoshiko blinked, took in Jenna's disheveled appearance, and the cut on her lip, and her anger seemed to drain away.

"Jenna?" she asked, her voice rising with concern. She jumped down from the top bunk. "What happened?" Yoshiko asked as she came across the room and reached out for her.

Jenna hugged Yoshiko tightly and began to cry, and all her fear poured out of her in a rush. If those medical students hadn't appeared when they had, she knew she might be dead now.

It would be a long while before she could push that out of her mind long enough to fall asleep. And she knew that, when she finally did, there would be nightmares.

Outside Sparrow Hall, on the lush lawn, the man in the hooded sweatshirt stood hidden among the pine trees.

He had an excellent view of Jenna's window.

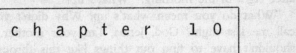

c h a p t e r   1 0

Jenna woke abruptly to the sound of the phone ringing. For the first few moments, she only lay there, blinking, trying to figure out who she was and where she'd been sleeping. *Okay. School. Somerset.*

Duh.

She groaned as the phone rang again, and forced herself to roll out from under the covers. Jenna yawned and stretched, stiff from her fall the night before, and felt a twinge of pain in her knee. She didn't even want to look at the bruise she knew must have blossomed there. On the top bunk, Yoshiko mumbled something unintelligible in her sleep and pulled her pillow over her head. Her eyes only half open, Jenna walked stiffly to the far wall and lifted the portable off its cradle just as the answering machine clicked on.

"Hang on," she drawled, then cleared her throat. She clicked the machine's "stop" button. "Hello?"

"Jenna."

"Hi, Mom," she croaked, glancing at the clock. Just after eight in the morning. "What's up?"

"What do you mean what's up? Why didn't you call me last night? God, Jenna, I'm your mother. I shouldn't have to find out things like this through early-morning phone calls from your *father.*"

Jenna blinked, really waking up at last. The word "father" had slipped out of her mother's mouth as though it were something that tasted awful. It had been a long time since Jenna had heard that tone in April's voice. But she knew it wasn't her dad's fault.

It was hers.

"Mom, I'm sorry. It was all just so crazy, you know? By the time I got back from the police station, and then . . . I was just so tired and fried. And, y'know, I'm fine. I fell down, but other than that, I'm really fine. He didn't lay a hand on me."

There was a long silence on the other end of the line. At length, she heard her mother inhale and exhale quickly, as though the breath were a punctuation of some sort.

"I want you to come home," April said.

Eyes wide, Jenna held the phone away from her head and stared at it half a second. Then she put it to her ear again. "Huh?"

"You heard me. This is insane. You've been through so much, so fast. Too much, Jenna. You saw your professor drop dead in front of you, not to mention kill that boy. This job you have . . . I don't think I like it. And now you have some kind of stalker."

A chill ran through her as she worried that her mother was right. Worried that she really did have a stalker—even if that stalker was a political assassin. But she wasn't about to let her mom know that.

"He wasn't stalking me, Mom," Jenna protested. "He was just some creep, he followed me, maybe he wanted a date or something. Besides, attacks like that take place every day on campuses all over the country. Anywhere I go, the same thing might have happened.

"And I happen to like my job," she said. "A lot. Yeah, it's weird, but it's medicine. I thought you'd be happy with that."

"I'm happy when you're safe. When I feel like you're in danger, then it doesn't matter if you're Surgeon General."

This time, it was Jenna who paused. She turned and leaned against the cinder block wall, up too early to be arguing with her mother. Yoshiko was sitting up in bed, looking at her with sympathetic eyes. Jenna shook her head and Yoshiko smiled.

"I'm not coming home, Mom. I'm staying in school. I'm not quitting and I'm not running away because some moron with weird ideas about how to get a date decides to see how fast I can run the hundred."

"I'm coming up there tomorrow," her mother said. "We're going to talk about this some more."

"If that will make you feel better, fine, but I'm not changing my mind. I'm not quitting," she repeated.

"Call your father," April replied, and this time, there was less obvious distaste on that word. "He spoke to Dr. Slikowski this morning. He wants to talk to you right away. Maybe he can talk some sense into you."

"I'll call," Jenna agreed.

"Jenna, be careful. It's possible this guy may be focused on you, even if he is just some pervert."

Bet on it, Jenna thought. But once again, she didn't express those thoughts to her mother. A moment later, both of them hung up, and Jenna went to lie back in bed. Before she could even pull the covers up, she noted the time again, and sighed heavily as she dragged herself from the mattress.

Yoshiko hung her head over the side of the top bunk, looking upside down at Jenna.

"You okay?" she asked.

Jenna thought about it for a moment. "I will be," she said. "Ask me again in a couple of days."

Breakfast with her father went only slightly better. When she'd called Frank, he was less worried than her mother had been. But he was also angrier. He hadn't cooled off that much when they met in front of the campus center and got in line for French toast.

"You should have called," he said sternly, trying fruitlessly to tuck in his rumpled shirt.

"I just wasn't thinking," Jenna replied with a shrug. "I'm sorry."

"You should be. I couldn't believe it when Walter told me. A parent should never have to find out something like this from someone else."

They quieted down as they stood in line to pass

their meal cards through, and then they found a table together.

"So, do you think I should leave, too?" she asked after a few quiet moments.

Her father looked up at her, eyebrows furrowed. "What?"

A student with a full breakfast tray bumped Jenna's chair. There was a low buzzing sound which was nothing more than the combined voices of all the students and professors who were inside talking and studying and eating and just living. The walls were tile, the floors were tile. The place was an echo chamber.

But he'd heard what she'd said, no question. Jenna didn't bother to repeat herself.

"No, I don't think you should leave," he explained. She waited for him to mention her mother, but he didn't. "There's no reason to believe it was anything but an isolated incident. But I do think you should think twice about walking around campus late at night by yourself. The school runs a safety shuttle on campus after dark. You could have called them."

Jenna thought about that, and had to nod in agreement. "You're right. I should have."

"Just be aware, watch where you're going. Try not to be out alone," her father said. He reached out to take her hand. "Your mother and I are both frightened for you, that's all. Even if that guy wasn't specifically after you, he's still out there. He'll go after some other girl. But as long as he's loose, there's a chance he'll be back, that you'll see him again."

Jenna blinked, looked away. "Wow. Way uplifting, padre."

"It's not meant to be uplifting, Jenna," he said, all stern again. "It's meant to scare you into being more careful."

After that, they ate their breakfast in relative peace. Several other faculty members came by the table to say hi to her father, and Jenna saw a few kids she knew from class. All the while, she was thinking about the things she'd told Mariano. Her suspicions. And as she did, she grew angrier and angrier.

Slick had told her father what had happened the night before. He had to have learned it from Gaines and Mariano. But her parents knew nothing about Jenna's suspicions, which meant that Mariano hadn't said a word about them. *Probably too embarrassed,* Jenna thought. And it *was* a little far-fetched. She could understand Mariano not wanting to be made to look foolish if she were wrong.

But I'm not wrong. I know it.

So far, Jenna had figured she'd been handling college pretty well. The classes were more difficult, more intense, but also a lot more interesting. It was easier to learn Spanish, for instance, in a "lecture room" with twenty other students who wanted to be there, than in a high school classroom with forty-five kids, half of whom couldn't care less.

She was loving college.

But Jenna had to admit, if only to herself, that Somerset looked a bit different to her after what had happened the night before. Still, despite her wariness, the day went along fine.

When she went to work afterward, however, things were quite awkward. She walked into the office to find Dyson doing some reports.

"Oh, hey, you all right?" he asked, his face showing his genuine concern.

"I'm fine," she said, blowing it off completely. "What's on the agenda for today?"

Dyson raised his eyebrows. "Hey, Jenna, really. Are you okay?"

She met his gaze. "I'm fine, Al, but thank you for worrying."

"Okay," he shrugged. "Look, don't stay late tonight. I'll make sure you get out of here on time."

Jenna smiled. That suited her just fine.

"So where's Dr. Slikowski today?" she asked.

"He's doing an autopsy right now. Got an intern down there helping him out. I was just helping him with a feasibility study we're doing on adding another autopsy room, and a staff pathologist. Since Slick is out and about as the county's M.E., it only makes sense."

"And you'd be staff pathologist, right?" she asked, raising an eyebrow and grinning.

Dyson got a sheepish look on his face. "Well, yeah."

"That'd be cool," she told him. "Good luck."

Nearly two hours later, the door opened, and Slick rolled in, a Walkman in his lap and earphones on his head. Jenna could hear wild jazz percussion streaming out. *And if I can hear it over here, how loud does he have that thing up?* This was a quirk of Slick's she'd been unaware of, and she scrutinized him a moment, as if seeing him for the first time. *Maybe he's not as stiff as he seems.*

His lanky frame bent over the wheels of his chair, and he maneuvered it around and into his office with barely a glance at either Jenna or Dyson.

Inside the door, he turned to look at her, slipped off the headphones, and clicked off the Walkman.

"You're not hurt, then?" he asked.

"Just a few bruises," she replied.

"Excellent," Dr. Slikowski told her. "Keep up the good work," he said, and then he closed his door, and stayed within his office, working, for the balance of the day. From time to time, Jenna could hear that jazz going again.

"He was worried about you," Dyson told her a short time later, when he caught Jenna staring at Slick's door. "I know it's hard to tell, but he definitely was."

"I'm okay," she insisted again.

It shouldn't have mattered whether Slick was worried about her or not, but strangely, it did. He was always busy with something—consulting with the police about forensic evidence, testifying at trials, performing autopsies at Somerset or one of the many hospitals in the county he represented as medical examiner. Colleagues from around the world called on him for his opinion. Jenna had quickly learned how well respected Dr. Walter Slikowski was in his field.

She sort of *had* to respect him for all of that. But he'd been kind to her, and could even be funny, in a very dry way, though she wasn't ever sure if he was actually aware of it.

Now the jazz. So he has a life outside of being the universe's foremost authority on all things dead. Jenna had already started to grow fond of Dr. Slikowski, but now he'd not only inquired after her health, but proven himself to have a bit more personality than she'd thought him capable of.

Which made her feel even more guilty about using his credentials to officially request the report from the autopsy of that reporter, Bernadette Knapp. All afternoon, she kept checking her e-mail to see if anything had come through.

By the time she left—after responding to a lot of Slick's correspondence and transcribing the tapes from two autopsies—she still hadn't received the information she wanted.

Dyson walked her back to the main campus, and she studied with Yoshiko and Hunter for a while before Melody showed up, fresh from her callback auditions for *The Sound of Music*. She was obviously replaying her performance in her head, but downplayed her anxiety, probably because she knew Jenna's mind was elsewhere. Jenna wanted to talk with her more, but she felt too distracted by her own whirling thoughts.

The four of them settled down and watched a movie together. Jenna was still exhausted, but she wasn't really tired. Even when she finally went to sleep, her mind was spinning once more.

Everything seemed wrong. Something was haunting her.

She slept.

But not for very long. After one in the morning, she woke to find Yoshiko fast asleep above her. There were sounds from the hallway, as usual. Some of her dorm-mates were still up, studying or partying or just hanging out. Big surprise. It wasn't *that* late.

She rolled over and tried to get back to sleep, and just couldn't manage it. Everything was a distraction. Even the moonlight streaming through the window.

Jenna flipped her pillow over, trying to keep the thickest part under her head. She lay on her back, unable to find a comfortable position in which to drift back to sleep.

Ah, who am I kidding? She was wide awake now. And who could blame her, after all she'd been through just in the past week and a half. Everything was a distraction tonight. Yoshiko's gentle breathing seemed too loud. The ticking of the comedy/tragedy mask clock her mother had bought her the previous Christmas was a constant reminder that she had biology class at ten minutes to nine the next day. And it was too bright in the room.

The moonlight.

Her mind instructed her body to get up out of bed and pull down the shades. Her body wasn't cooperating. Instead, she turned onto her side and tried again to find a comfortable position.

For several minutes she lay with her eyes tightly closed, trying to fool her mind into believing that she was sleepy. No luck. Exhausted, yes, but she was definitely not sleepy. So, instead of sleeping, she lay there and felt sorry for herself.

Though she'd kept telling everyone she was all right, she had bruises on her face and arms and a big one on her hip from the fall the night before. They were all very sore. She was trying to lie on her left side, because the right was too tender. It wasn't just the bruises, though. She was haunted by the memory of the man in the hood.

The man without a face.

She knew there was something major going on. Something horrible. She knew it had to have something to do with Carlos Gutierrez and Costa Rica, or at least, she was pretty sure of it. But who was doing the killing, and how were they pulling it off?

Her mind raced. Eventually, it came to a stop on Danny Mariano. She understood his attitude, but it didn't stop her from feeling pretty angry about it.

Then there was a small fact that she'd only begun to really deal with, even recognize, tonight while she and her friends were watching their movie.

Jenna thought she had a crush on the detective. Never mind that he was at least ten, maybe even fifteen years older than she was. Never mind that they'd only met a couple of times. There was just something about him, a kind of energy and confidence. *And, okay, he's a muffin.* But there was a lot more to him than just that.

And it didn't hurt that she thought it was pretty obvious he liked her. Not that anything could ever happen. She was sure nothing ever would. But for a little while tonight, it had been fun to think about, sort of a delicious little thrill that she could enjoy just in her own head. He'd been really nice to her, worried about her, drove her home.

But he'd pretty much blown her off.

Oh, he'd been all concerned about her being attacked, worried about her safety and all that. In its way, that was sort of nice. But Jenna was no damsel in distress. She was never going to be that. If Danny had a knight-in-shining-armor syndrome or something, well, that was his thing, not hers. Whatever it was, when Jenna had started to explain her suspicions to Danny, he'd brushed them off as just too wild.

She was an eighteen-year-old girl, barely out of high school. What did she know?

Plenty. And one of the things she knew was that, no matter how smart he was, no matter how cute he was, Jenna was going to forget all about Danny Mariano. She was going to put him out of her mind completely, and concentrate on what was really going on around here. It seemed like nobody could figure out why people were dying. Or nobody was talking about it. The woman from CDC was only thinking about the supergerm. The FBI was only in on it because of the dead congressional aide. And Slick . . . he just couldn't make the leap to connect it all. It was too far-fetched for his logical mind.

Danny was her best bet, and if he didn't believe her . . .

Oh, would you stop thinking about him! she snapped silently at herself. *Go to sleep!*

Which was easier said than done.

Still, somehow, just before two in the morning, Jenna finally began to drift off. The waves of adrenaline that had washed over her had receded at last, and gradually, she surrendered to sleep. Slowly, her conscious thoughts gave way to the nonsense that churned in her dreams. As she slipped away, she thought again of the man who had attacked her, the shadow of a face in the dark, hidden by that hood. That cruel, guttural voice.

With you out of the way, it'll all be taken care of.

Jenna's eyes snapped open and she stared at the intricate wire webbing that held Yoshiko's mattress above her.

The words played in her head again. "It'll all be taken care of," Jenna whispered to herself. "Oh my God."

Jenna whipped the covers back, swung her legs out, and got one of her feet tangled in the spread, nearly tumbling to the throw rug her mother had bought for the cold dorm floor.

"Oh my God!" she repeated, shouting this time.

While Jenna struggled to calm down long enough to get both legs into her blue jeans, Yoshiko poked her head over the edge of the top bunk. Her hair was wildly mussed, and she blinked blearily, trying to focus her vision.

"Hey, J," she croaked. "What's going on?"

"Go back to sleep, Yoshiko," Jenna said, pulling her sneakers over the socks she'd worn to bed. "It's . . . it's probably nothing."

But now Yoshiko was awake enough to see how frantic her roommate was, and Jenna wasn't going to get away with a brush-off.

"Jenna." Yoshiko slid over the edge of the bunk and dropped to the floor. "What's wrong? Another . . . has somebody else died?"

As she bunched up her nightshirt to tuck it into her jeans, Jenna met Yoshiko's questioning gaze. She paused, took a breath, and then let the fear that had been building inside her rush at last to the surface. She swallowed, began to breathe in ragged gasps, and fought away the tears that threatened as her eyes welled with moisture.

"It's my dad," she said, her voice breaking.

"He's not . . ." Yoshiko began, but couldn't bring herself to say the word "dead." Instead, she frowned. "But I didn't even hear the phone ring."

Jenna shook her head, searching the room for her jacket.

"He's not dead," she said. "At least not yet. But remember I told you the guy who attacked me, he said that after he killed me, it would be taken care of. I think he meant the threat to Carlos Gutierrez."

"Well, yeah," Yoshiko said. "I mean, if you're right about that aide and Professor Mattei being killed because of Gutierrez, and then you were snooping around . . . well, what else would he mean?"

Then the girl's beautiful brown eyes widened in sudden understanding and alarm.

"If Gutierrez knows my dad's been trying to finish Professor Mattei's work, then my father would be a target, too," Jenna explained.

Yoshiko was already reaching for the suede pants she'd worn that day, for once not paying attention to whether or not her outfit was going to look good.

"And if the guy who jumped you said it was over, that would mean they've already gotten to him," Yoshiko said, as she slipped on her brown shoes. "Poisoned him or something, something that would take some time to . . ."

Yoshiko looked up and stared at her roommate in horror. She'd finally figured out what Jenna was so terrified about. They'd both seen Jenna's dad that day, and he'd looked fine.

But if they'd put one of those disgusting insects in his ear, it could have laid its eggs by now. They could hatch at any time. And when they did, it would be too late. Frank Logan would go mad.

Then he would die.

"God," Yoshiko whispered. "You'd better call that detective."

"He doesn't believe me," Jenna said bitterly, fighting her fear.

Then she grabbed her jacket and pulled open the door.

"Come on," she said. "I've finally got a chance to know my father. I'm not going to let him die now."

chapter 11

Jenna shot out the front door of Sparrow Hall and down the brick steps, heart pounding wildly in her chest. Yoshiko came up beside her and, together, they sprinted across the quad to Fletcher Avenue. The campus was eerie this time of night. Not deserted; not exactly. But Jenna could hear sounds of laughter from far off, and across the quad she saw a small knot of shadowy figures moving across the lawn. The Civil War cannon next to the chapel was receiving a paint job from a pair of girls she didn't recognize. At least twice a week, someone painted the cannon with a slogan or a political statement or just to do it.

There was no humor in it tonight.

The street lamps were too far apart. Their illumination provided only pools of light, safe haven between the shadows that seemed to be eating the available light. This was something she'd never had occasion to notice before; and now, she only noticed because it

176

gave her something to focus on. Something to keep her mind away from her belief that her father had been . . . *what?*

Infected. Somehow, she now believed, he must have been infected by the same disease that had already driven at least two men mad, not to mention killed them.

She wasn't going to let that happen.

In and out of the splashes of light thrown by the inadequate streetlights, Jenna and Yoshiko ran on in silence. What could they have said to one another? Nothing. Still, Jenna was glad to have her there. Glad that she wasn't alone for once. She had felt more and more isolated by her job—and how odd everyone thought it was—and the mystery that it seemed only she saw as real.

They passed the tennis courts, and Jenna started to breathe hard. Yoshiko seemed fine, and Jenna felt a flash of envy. Then it was gone, as she pounded down the broken sidewalk to the intersection where Fletcher crossed Sterling and continued on the other side as Lewis Street. Across Sterling, Jenna could see that the windows were dark in the house her father shared only with Shayna Emerson, now that their other housemate, Professor Mattei, was dead.

A small whimper escaped Jenna's lips as she started across the street. She didn't think she could go any faster, but somehow, she managed. A moment later, she bounded up the wooden steps of the old house, and Yoshiko ran up behind her.

There were three doorbells. Jenna pushed the middle one, held it down for several seconds, and then let it up. She waited: one, two, three, four . . . and pushed it again. Still nothing.

"Jenna," Yoshiko said gently, and laid a hand on Jenna's shoulder.

"Ohgod. Come on, Daddy. Come on," she chanted, mostly to herself. She bounced on the balls of her feet as though she were cold. The adrenaline pumped through her body, and she wanted to scream.

Her finger stabbed the doorbell again, and this time, she held the buzzer down and refused to let it up. Five, six, seven, eight, twelve, thirteen—

"This better be good," the gruff voice of Frank Logan crackled on the little speaker above the buttons.

Yoshiko gripped Jenna's shoulder.

"Oh, thank God," Jenna whispered to herself. Then she spoke up. "Dad, it's me. I have to talk to you."

The door buzzed instantly.

Jenna pushed the door open, and Yoshiko followed her in. She started up the steps as fast as she could without making a thundering racket that she feared would wake Shayna. Before she reached the second-floor landing, she heard her father call her name. Jenna looked up to see him staring down at her, a slightly ragged terrycloth robe belted around his waist. The corners of his eyes were crinkled, his brow creased with concern. He was afraid for her.

She'd expected him to be angry, or at least a bit annoyed that she'd showed up at his door at quarter past two in the morning. Now, Jenna realized that she ought to have known better. Tired or not, woken up in the middle of the night or not, she'd been attacked a little more than twenty-four hours earlier. Her father's sole concern was for her safety.

"Dad," she said, her voice cracking with emotion. He was worried about her, when he was the one in the most danger.

"Jenna, honey, what's going on?" Frank asked anxiously.

She reached the landing and threw her arms around him, drew him close in an embrace unlike any they'd shared in years. His being an absentee father had put space between them that she hadn't thought would ever go away. And maybe it would always be there. But in that one moment, there were no lingering feelings of guilt or anger to separate father and daughter.

Only love. And fear.

"Hello, Professor Logan," Yoshiko said quietly.

"Hi, Yoshiko," Jenna's dad replied. "Now, assuming you two didn't wake me up to try to get Yoshiko an extension on the paper she owes me next week, why don't you tell me what all this is about."

Jenna pushed away from her father and looked up into his face.

"Are you all right?" she asked. "I mean, do you feel all right?"

Frank Logan smiled. "Well, other than a little disorientation from being woken in the middle of the night, I'm fine. Why?"

His daughter stared into his eyes. "You're sure?" Jenna asked. "Not feeling wigged at all? No violent tendencies?"

Frank blinked several times. "Jenna, what's all this about?"

Yoshiko looked from Jenna to her father and back again. "Jenna, he seems fine," she said. "I mean, he'd be feeling weird, right? That's how it works? But he's not, y'know, breaking furniture or anything."

With a long sigh, Jenna said, "Maybe I'm just psycho." Then she looked up at her father quickly, apologetically, and added, "Not that I want anything to happen to you. I was just completely freaked. I probably should have just called, but you live right down the street, and I had to see you for myself, to know you were really all right. See, the guy, the one who attacked me? He said that when he was done with me—"

Frank had been glancing down the steps. Now he interrupted.

"You know, girls, why don't we talk about this inside. I'd hate to wake Shayna."

Jenna's mind was spinning as she and Yoshiko followed her father inside his apartment. In the living room, she sat down on one arm of the sofa, and Yoshiko dropped into an old rocker.

"I'm going to put water on for tea," Frank said. "I have a feeling this is going to be a long night. Anyone else want some?"

Both girls passed. When Frank walked out of the room, Yoshiko looked at Jenna.

"He looks fine," she said again.

"I know," Jenna replied, nodding. "It's just . . . I was so sure. I mean, if I'm right about all of this crazy business . . . they know about me, right? Well, they must be looking into what Professor Mattei did with his research. They have to know about my dad helping finish it up."

"Or maybe they don't," Yoshiko replied. "Maybe that's why he said it would be over with you. On the other hand . . ."

Her words trailed off, and Yoshiko just kind of shrugged. It was obvious she didn't want to say it, but Jenna knew what was on her mind. Yoshiko had been about to bring up the possibility that all of Jenna's suspicions were nothing more than paranoia. That it was just a matter for CDC, just something natural but deadly, making its way out of the rain forest for the first time.

In some ways, that would be worse. You could stop a person from doing something awful, Jenna knew, but there isn't much you could do about nature if it got nasty.

She was still pretty confident that her suspicions were correct. She couldn't imagine that the attack on her the night before was just random violence. *Not with the way the guy talked to me.* Maybe they just didn't know about her dad yet.

Yet. She was going to have to get to the bottom of this, and sooner rather than later.

"Maybe we should go," Jenna suggested sheepishly.

"Sleep is good," Yoshiko replied.

"Sleep is good," Jenna agreed. "But like most things, vastly overrated."

The teakettle whistled for just a moment, and Jenna

glanced toward the kitchen. She sighed again and pushed away from the sofa.

"Sorry I dragged you out of bed," she told her roommate.

"Please," Yoshiko said, lifting her eyebrows. "I'm just glad you were wrong."

Jenna smiled wearily, and walked into the kitchen. Her father was pouring hot water into a mug. The string and tag from a teabag lay over the edge of the mug like an anchor. Frank put the pot down and stirred some milk into his tea. He stuck a finger into his left ear and twisted it around.

"Dad, listen, we're going back to the dorm," Jenna said. "I'm sorry I woke you up. I think all of this stuff has me jumping at shadows or whatever. I want to talk to you about it—about all the things I think are happening—but it'll keep until morning."

Frank sipped his tea, sighed miserably. "You've got me up now, *daughter*. You're not even going to see what's on the late late show with me?"

"Not even," Jenna replied. "Father."

She smiled at him, and Frank smiled back. He took another sip of his tea, and then made a face. Stuck his pinky finger into his ear again and twisted it like he was mixing cake batter.

Jenna was about to say good-bye, but something stopped her. She watched her father, watched his face.

She stopped breathing for a second.

When she started again, she shouted. "Yoshiko!"

Over his mug of tea, Frank frowned at his daughter. "Jenna," he began, "Shayna's sleeping down—"

Yoshiko shot into the kitchen. Jenna saw the worry in her face, and knew it was just a reflection of her own.

"Call the hospital!" Jenna snapped. "Tell them to get Dr. Slikowski and have him meet us there!"

As Yoshiko ran back into the living room, where a portable phone sat on a small wooden table, Jenna reached out and grabbed her father's hand, and gave him a yank. Hot tea sloshed over his other hand and spilled onto his robe and the floor.

"Jenna, what the hell's gotten into you?" he said angrily, kind of hissing as he put his mug on the kitchen counter.

She blinked. She'd thought he understood. "Get your pants on, Dad. Now, please. I don't know how much time we have. We have to—"

"Time for what?" he demanded.

"Your ear," she said. "How long's it been bothering you?"

As if on cue, he began to scratch at his inner ear again. He stared at her as though she were insane.

"Just since you woke me," Frank replied. "Will you tell me what's—"

"I think it's one of those bugs," she said quickly. "With the germ that killed José."

Her father's eyes widened. Then, looking slightly stunned, he began to move toward his bedroom. He slipped into pants and shoes quickly, and when they passed Yoshiko in the living room, on the phone with the hospital, Frank Logan was nearly running.

He was running for his life. And Jenna was right there with him.

"There's *something* in there, all right," Dr. Heckler said, as she pointed a pencil-beam flashlight into Frank's ear. "It's very red, and it looks as though there's a small hole. Like a tick has burrowed under the skin or something."

"Oh my God," Jenna whispered, her eyes wide with fear as she watched the doctor examine her father.

Frank looked terrified as well, and he reached out to clutch his daughter's hands in his own.

Dr. Heckler, despite her odd name, seemed to be very professional and very confident. She was on call at the hospital, and had confirmed as they arrived that Dr. Slikowski had been called and was on his way. If it hadn't been for the fact that Jenna worked for him, they never would have bothered to call, Dr. Heckler explained.

Jenna had been relieved. But that hadn't lasted long. Not now that she knew she'd been right.

"I don't understand," her father said suddenly. "I mean, how did it get in there?"

"Someone put it there, Dad," Jenna said.

"What?" he asked doubtfully. "Why would anyone do such a thing?"

"Because you're trying to finish Professor Mattei's papers," she said hurriedly, so tired of having to try to explain her theories. *But they don't sound so crazy anymore, do they?* she thought. "I'll bet it was the same guy who came after me last night. They figured a campus attack wouldn't be at all suspicious if I got killed. But with that Garson guy, and José, and now with you, they've *used* this bug. Somehow, they've got to get to you, while you're sleeping or something, and slip it in there."

"This is all so insane," Jenna's father said. But he didn't question her again.

It was quiet in the ER that night. A student was having a gash in his arm stitched up in one room, and that was about it. That, and Jenna's father, who sat very quietly as he waited to find out if he was going to die. A few minutes later, the double doors at the end of the ER hallway swung open, and Dr. Slikowski guided his wheelchair into the sterile corridor.

Slick wheeled his chair over and had Frank squat down so he could have a look with the penlight as well. His finely boned face looked extra severe, and he clucked under his tongue. Then he handed Dr. Heckler back her light, and removed his wire-rim glasses. He held them on his lap as he blinked several times and looked up at Jenna and her father.

The M.E.'s eyes rested on Frank Logan.

"You've really stepped into it this time, Frank," he said.

Jenna sucked in a breath and bit her lip. Slick glanced over at her, and seemed about to speak when the double doors swung wide again. Jenna looked up to see FBI Agent Jeffries and Dr. Martin from the CDC coming down the corridor at a fast pace.

"What've we got here, Doc?" Jeffries asked grumpily.

He looked as though he'd just rolled out of bed. So did Dr. Martin for that matter. Jenna felt silly when she realized that, more than likely, that's exactly what had happened.

"Well, Agent Jeffries, it seems we have a mystery on our hands. Even greater than the one we thought we were dealing with," Dr. Slikowski replied.

"Walter . . ." Jenna's father began.

"God, could you guys please talk about all this later and save my father's life first?" Jenna snapped, glaring around at them each in turn, waiting for someone to challenge her.

No one did.

"I've done a bit of research since all this began," Slick announced. "If this insect is anything like the botfly, and we have every reason to believe it is, we must be careful while extracting it. If it breaks, we may leave the egg sac behind, which will then be almost impossible to remove."

"So how do you get it out?" Dr. Heckler asked.

Jenna had nearly forgotten the woman was there. Now she merely nodded in agreement.

Slick reached inside his coat and from an inner pocket produced a thick strip of frozen bacon wrapped in plastic. He handed it over to Dr. Heckler. "Would you mind heating this in the microwave in the doctors' lounge?" he asked.

Heckler stared at him. So did everyone else for that matter.

Dr. Slikowski slipped his glasses back on, and ran his fingers through his graying hair. "Please, Doctor. I'll explain as we go."

The process was actually pretty repulsive. It seemed that this insect, which had yet to receive a name, if similar enough to the botfly, would continue to nibble a hole in the skin to allow air in. If Frank held the warm bacon to his ear long enough, pressed tightly enough, the bug would dig itself out, then begin to burrow through the bacon. Once it made an opening on the other side, they could simply pull the bacon away and the bug would come with it.

"Let's try not to kill it, please," Dr. Martin said. "It will make it much easier to search for a cure for this supergerm if we have a sample that hasn't been squashed underfoot."

"If that's where the disease is coming from," grumbled Agent Jeffries, still annoyed about losing sleep.

"It seems unlikely at this point that it could have come from anywhere else," Dr. Martin replied. "In addition, a live sample will be of great use to the entomologist I've been in contact with."

While the group stood around chatting about science, and Frank Logan held a piece of bacon to his ear, complaining loudly about how badly it itched him as the bug dug its way out, Jenna prayed that her father wasn't going to die. She sat in a hard chair for a while, and began to fall asleep with her head back against the wall.

She didn't realize she actually had closed her eyes until she heard a distant voice speak her name.

Her eyelids fluttered.

"Jenna?" the voice said again.

She opened her eyes, began to yawn and stretch as she focused on the face in front of her. Danny Mariano. She blinked, stopped stretching, and pulled the yawn back in as best she could. She blushed a bit, then frowned.

"What are you doing down here?" she asked him.

Before Danny could answer, his partner, Audrey Gaines, approached. "Your roommate called looking for Detective Mariano," she said. "It looks like there's a lot more going on here than some kind of disease."

Jenna nodded slowly. Then she realized that Audrey and Danny weren't the only people looking at her. They all were. Agent Jeffries and Dr. Martin. Even Slick was looking at her, eyebrows raised in speculation. Her father lay on a gurney against the far wall, bacon still pressed against his ear.

"Okay, now I know how a lab specimen feels," she said sheepishly. "Anyone care to talk, or are you all zombies now?"

"I think you're right," Danny said suddenly.

It was Jenna's turn to stare.

"I still think this whole thing is nuts," Dr. Martin interrupted. "First, you'd have to have the science to genetically engineer the germ, and then find or engineer the perfect host insect to carry it. Then you'd have to have a human who would knowingly be the delivery system, placing the insects in the ears of the intended victims. No insect is going to go there directly, no matter how much genetic tampering has been done. And they certainly can't be trained.

"Who the hell would do something like that?" she asked, incredulous.

"You'd be surprised," Agent Jeffries told her, then glanced around at the rest of them. "I've heard stories about even crazier ways people have committed murder. And, let's face it, if the deaths hadn't been so close together, it would still seem like an awful coincidence. I mean, there've been some pretty nasty outbreaks of supergerms before, and no one's shouted conspiracy. Except the people who do it all the time."

Jenna blinked, shook her head, and sat up straighter in her chair. "I don't get it," she said. "You all thought it was just coincidence before. But this was enough to convince you?"

"That, and the attack on you Monday night," Danny replied.

"And one other small thing," Slick interjected.

Jenna looked at him, and for the first time, she thought he looked rather small in his chair. But in spite of that, he still had a powerful presence. His was probably the sharpest mind there.

"The reporter from D.C., Bernadette Knapp? I received her autopsy report last night," Dr. Slikowski explained. "She died the same way Mr. Garson and Professor Mattei did."

"I know I shouldn't have made an official request for—" Jenna began.

"It's a good thing you did," he interrupted. "There are still a lot of pieces missing here."

"Not to mention a killer on the loose, and no real way to tie him to Carlos Gutierrez," Detective Gaines added.

"There's something else," Jenna's father interjected.

They all turned to look at him, and Jenna felt sort of embarrassed for him. He looked pretty silly with Dr. Heckler holding a slab of meat over his ear. But the expression on his face, a mixture of regret and anger, erased any temptation she might have had to laugh or even smile.

"What is it, Professor?" Audrey asked.

"Monday morning, before I left for class, I couldn't find the folder where I had most of my paperwork on the Gutierrez situation. Of course, I have it all on computer, on disks, and backup disks, and now I'm certainly going to make a copy. At the time, I assumed I'd misplaced it. I didn't remember moving it from the desk, but it wouldn't be the first time. I can be sort of absentminded that way.

"Then, after what happened to Jenna, I was a bit preoccupied, and I knew I had it on the computer. My report is substantially complete. So I brushed it off, assuming I'd find it later. Now I know better."

"So he knew what he was looking for?" Danny wondered aloud.

"Not necessarily," Jenna replied. "That folder was on top of the desk. Once he'd put that disgusting thing in my father's ear, the guy must have looked around, found the folder, and grabbed it."

"Why didn't he just destroy the computer, take the disks, all of that?" Dr. Martin asked.

"He's attempting to be surreptitious about things," Dr. Slikowski said, sliding his wheelchair back a bit, looking around at those gathered. "Why, until today, none of us really believed any of this except for Jenna. On Monday, our killer thought he had it all under control. Put our little viral bug in Professor Logan's ear and attack Jenna on campus. If he'd done anything obvious at the professor's apartment, it would have tipped him off that someone had been there. The bug might not have had time to lay its eggs. It didn't matter to him if the records were on the computer. Once Jenna and her father were dead, with no one believing there was any kind of conspiracy, it would have been all over, wouldn't it?"

Slick looked kindly at Jenna. "But Jenna wasn't going down that easily, were you? Not only did you escape him, but you figured out what he'd been up to and managed to reach your father in time. Well done, Jenna."

She blushed deeply.

Suddenly, Dr. Heckler interrupted with a loud "Yes!"

They all looked over at her. She held the strip of bacon in a specimen cup. When Jenna got close enough, she could see it there, on the bacon. The tiny, greenish-white, wormlike thing that had almost killed her father.

Frank sat up on the gurney.

"How are you feeling?" Slick asked him.

"Like I'm going to throw up," Jenna's dad replied. "But it's just nerves, I think."

"Still, let's make sure that thing didn't have time to lay its eggs," Dr. Slikowski said. Then he looked over at Dr. Heckler. "And let's do a full workup to make sure there are no traces of this disease left behind, all right?"

Jenna's heart sank. More waiting. She didn't think she could wait anymore. She just wanted to know that her dad was all right, that he was going to live, not go berserk and then . . . die. Like José Mattei. She flashed on that horrible afternoon suddenly, and felt her eyes well with tears.

"Jenna, he'll be all right."

She looked up to see Danny Mariano. He was the only one who'd noticed her distress. He laid a hand on her shoulder and squeezed a moment before letting go.

"He's gonna be all right," Danny said again.

Jenna went to her father then. He smiled and opened his arms and took her in a firm embrace.

"My little girl," he said. "And you saved my life."

Jenna didn't say anything to that. She couldn't. Not until she was sure he was truly going to be all right. And it would be hours before they had that information.

"Go home and get some sleep," Slick told her.

She turned to face him, saw her own anxiety in his face, and nodded slightly.

"Thanks for coming down," she told him.

"Thanks for seeing something the rest of us missed," he replied. "Or just weren't willing to consider. Why don't you come by the office about four o'clock? We'll have a lot to talk about later."

"Including how to protect you and your dad," Danny added.

Jenna shivered. She realized she would have to help her father with Professor Mattei's papers. Not to mention trying to figure out who had attacked her. She didn't have a choice. Not if she wanted to live.

As long as the killer was still on the loose, as long as Gutierrez's secrets remained secrets, they would never be safe again.

chapter 12

When the knock came at the door to her room, Jenna had been sleeping for just over four hours. Not enough. Not by a long shot. But apparently, it was going to have to do.

Forcing her eyes to open, she whipped back the covers and stumbled from bed. On the top bunk, Yoshiko was still sleeping. She'd pulled a pillow over her head, and Jenna mentally cursed herself for not thinking of the old pillow maneuver herself.

"All right!" Jenna snapped at the mad knocker. "The meteor isn't gonna hit in the next thirty seconds."

Grumbling, wiping sleep from her eyes, and too tired to be self-conscious about the fact that she didn't have anything on but her underwear and a Superman T-shirt, she pulled the door open.

"What?" she sighed.

Jenna looked up to see her mother staring back at

her. The look on April Blake's face was anything but amused. But it wasn't exactly angry, either. In fact, if Jenna had to describe the look on her mom's face at that precise moment, she figured she'd have to go with panicked.

Panicked. Yeah. That was about right.

"Hi, Mom," Jenna said, with less humor than she was trying for. "In the neighborhood?"

April pushed past Jenna into the room, glanced up to see Yoshiko sleeping, and then let out a long breath, as though she'd been holding it. She still hadn't said a word.

"Mom?"

"You were sleeping?" April asked.

Jenna hesitated. "I . . . didn't get much sleep last night. Neither one of us did."

April nodded, her lips pressed together so tightly that they formed a white line. "I understand you had a long night," her mother said. "I also understand you saved your father's life."

With a soft grunt, Jenna blinked. "Um, I guess I hadn't thought of it like that."

Her mother narrowed her eyes and gazed at Jenna sternly. "No, I guess you're not thinking about much of anything these past few days, are you?"

Hands on hips, Jenna protested. "That isn't fair, Mom. It isn't like I asked to be involved in this thing, you know. I don't have any choice now. Are you telling me being a surgeon has never put you in harm's way?"

"Not like this, Jenna, for God's sake!" her mother barked.

Yoshiko snuggled farther beneath her covers, her head still beneath her pillow.

"Mom," Jenna said calmly, "I've got this job now. Part of what Dr. Slikowski does is forensic investigation. But that isn't even it. Professor Mattei died, and I had to watch it happen. I wanted to know why. I wanted to know how."

"You don't have to keep the job."

Jenna shot her mother a withering glance. "I *like* my job. In fact, for once, I feel like maybe there is something out there for me to do, as an *adult*."

Glancing around the room as if she were looking for someone to help argue her case, April eventually threw up her hands and went to sit down at the chair in front of Jenna's desk. She reached out for a framed 5" x 7" of the two of them together at Jenna's high school graduation and ran her finger along the glass.

With a shake of her head, April turned to look at her daughter, eyes imploring.

"I'm not asking you to quit the job, Jenna," she said. "Not if you feel that strongly about it. All I want is for you to come home until all of this blows over. Until they get to the bottom of this. I mean, according to your father, you're a . . . God, I can't even believe I'm saying this. You're a target, Jenna. You've got to come home!"

Part of Jenna wanted to give in. Just to surrender to her mother's demands. She was April Blake's daughter, after all. Her mother had never really steered her wrong. They'd always been close, and April was only doing this because she was justifiably frightened about it all.

But she couldn't give in.

"Try to understand, Mom," she began, and saw the hopeful light in her mother's eyes snuffed out in an instant.

"Jenna—"

"Please, just let me talk," Jenna snapped. They stared at each other for a long, silent moment. Then she tried again. "If I am a target, then I'm a target at home, here at school, or at the top of Mount Everest. And don't forget that Dad's a target, too. I know you don't love him, but you can't want him dead. If I stay here, I have the FBI, the state police, and campus security watching out for me. Crazy as you may think it is, I'm actually safer here on campus than at home with you."

April looked insulted a moment, and then she just shook her head again and glanced away.

"Plus, I want to stay, Mom. I started to put this all together before anyone else. I've got to know how it ends. What I saw in the classroom that day with Professor Mattei—let's just say I want to make sure the man who caused that doesn't ever do it again.

"And they're close now. They know how it all happened, and they're pretty sure of why. It's just a matter of figuring out who did it all, whose hands actually committed the crimes."

The shadowed face of her hooded attacker flashed

in the back of Jenna's mind, but she shoved the memory away.

"I need to be here," Jenna said again. "It's safer. And it's something I have to see through."

And I'm not going to leave my father behind, she thought, but she didn't say it. She would never want her mother to get the idea that she was putting her father first. That just wasn't the case.

She was putting herself first.

April buried her face in her hands. In a harsh whisper, she said, "Jenna, if anything were to happen to you . . ."

"Nothing's going to happen, Mom. It's only a matter of time, now. Believe me. And I'm going to be very careful," Jenna promised.

Then she walked across the room to where her mother sat, and put her hand on April's shoulder. April turned and pulled her daughter into a tight embrace.

"Do you really think you're safer here?" she asked.

"I've got everyone involved in this case watching out for me and for Dad. We'll be fine. And once Dad releases the papers Professor Mattei was preparing when he died, there won't be any reason left to come after us."

For a long time, April only held her. Then, slowly, she drew back and stared into Jenna's eyes.

"I just . . . I'm on call the next few days, and I have a lot of operations scheduled. But I'll cancel it all."

"No," Jenna said quickly. "Don't do that, Mom."

April frowned. "Why on earth not?"

"Dad's a target. So am I. If you're around, this guy's going to make you a target, too, just assuming we've told you what we know."

Her mother grew pale, and Jenna hugged her more tightly. She was a bit embarrassed, knowing that Yoshiko was likely awake but pretending to sleep out of politeness.

Still, she held her mother for a long time.

A little after two o'clock, Jenna went over to the medical center. She wasn't supposed to meet with Slick and the police until four, but she wanted to see her father before then.

She was heartened to see that there was already a policeman on guard at his door. Jenna smiled at the guard, then knocked on the open door to her father's hospital room. Frank Logan looked up and smiled when he saw her.

"You got some sleep, I hope?" he asked.

"I'm all right," she replied. "I would have had more if Mom hadn't ambushed me. You called her, didn't you?"

Frank blinked. "Y'know, a 'how are you' might have been nice."

Jenna raised an eyebrow. "How're you feeling, Dad?"

He nodded. "It was kind of a long night. The talk shows they don't allow on during the day are on at four in the morning."

"But other than possible Ricki Lake-itis, you feel all

right?" Jenna prodded, as she walked over to sit down in an ugly brown leather chair.

Her father's gaze drifted suddenly, his eyes wandering as though he were avoiding looking at her. Jenna felt her stomach do a small acrobatic maneuver.

"Dad?"

He looked back at her. "I'm fine," he said. "Just nervous. The woman from CDC, what's her name? Dr. Martin. She said that insect *was* loaded with the same germ that killed José and the other man, Garson."

Jenna felt suddenly cold. Goosebumps appeared on her arms and a shiver ran through her. But she did not turn away from her father. She didn't even let her eyes wander. *Please, oh please . . .*

"Did she say if it laid its eggs?"

Frank smiled grimly, shrugged a little. "It didn't. No eggs. But there's still a chance I'll get it just from having the thing biting into my ear like that. Dr. Martin's happy to have a specimen, though. She says that with that, they might be able to come up with a cure. But I know a little about these supergerms. They mutate and become something else, even if CDC *can* find a cure."

Frowning, Jenna swallowed hard and reached out to touch her father's hand.

"It'll be all right, Dad. It's all good news so far, right?"

He nodded. "Right."

Jenna brightened. "So does that mean I can yell at you now about calling Mom?"

Frank grew serious again, his face taking on a grave expression. "I'll find out later today if I'm infected, Jenna. But I'm hanging over the edge, you know what I mean? Death is right around the corner, about to jump out at me and yell boo!"

"I think you should go home."

She could only stare at him. It was easy to understand her father's motivations. He was worried about a daughter he had only just begun to get to know. But understanding didn't mean she was going to agree.

"I've already been through this with Mom," she replied. "I'm not going to do it again. I love you. I know you're going to be all right. You'd better hurry up and get out of here, because if you don't, you're not going to be there to see it when they take the bastard down.

"I'm not going anywhere, Dad. That's it."

Jenna kissed her father's stubbly cheek and ignored his protests as she walked out of the hospital room.

She took the elevator to the second floor and walked down the long hall to Dr. Slikowski's office. When she walked in, Dyson was pulling on a white coat. Slick was in his office on the phone, but when he saw her, his eyes widened, he smiled kindly, and waved.

"You're early," Dyson noted as Jenna went to her cubicle.

"I've got a lot on my mind," she told him, and didn't elaborate.

"I don't blame you," Dyson told her.

Slick wheeled his chair out into the main office and

looked over at Jenna. His glasses reflected the fluorescent light at an odd angle, and for a moment, he looked vibrant. He even seemed to be excited, enthusiastic, though Jenna didn't understand why. But she suspected it was all of this, the mystery. It thrilled him, as gruesome as it all was.

She understood.

"Are you here to talk to the authorities, or to work?" Slick asked.

"Work."

The M.E. smiled. "We've got an autopsy right now. Supposedly, the subject was struck by a motorcyclist. Rather gruesome, actually. But if you think you're up to it, I could use your assistance."

"I'm your girl," Jenna assured him.

It was gruesome, as promised. The "subject" turned out to be a fifty-four-year-old woman named Naomi Mackeson, but with the damage done to her face and skull in the accident, she would be unrecognizable even to her family.

The three of them spent the better part of two hours on the autopsy, and that didn't account for the many subsequent tests that would be run as a matter of course. They found nothing that indicated that Mrs. Mackeson's death had occurred in any way other than circumstances seemed to indicate, but those subsequent tests could still reveal contributing factors. Establishing a cause of death in a case of violent death, Jenna had learned, was never as simple as a layman might think. For the M.E. to be certain, an autopsy must be performed.

For the first time, Jenna was required to actually lift out the organs herself—with Slick and Dyson's direction—and weigh and dissect them. Dyson gave her strict instruction on the dissection part.

With a web of Mrs. Mackeson's intestines in her hands, she looked over at Slick, astounded. "You can't tell me that this is something pathology assistants do on a regular basis. I mean, if there's something to be seen during these dissections, I'm not going to see it."

Dr. Slikowski smiled. "No, it isn't exactly par for the course," he admitted. "But you seemed to need a distraction as much as the rest of us. And there's no harm in learning, is there?"

Jenna blinked, her eyes wide. "No . . . I guess not."

She stared down into the empty cavern of jagged, shattered ribs that had once been a human being. The white of the bone, the almost artificial hue of the sliced flesh, both were in stark contrast to the darkness inside.

It should bother me. But it doesn't.

Suddenly, Jenna felt as though a burden had been lifted from her. She was repulsed by violence and death and the very concept of harm befalling those close to her, but she realized now that there was a dividing line between compassion and science. Ever since she'd first walked into this autopsy room, barely two weeks earlier, she'd been clumsily wandering about on that line without seeing it.

Now she saw it clearly. On one side were her expected emotional responses. On the other, the science of discovery, and the construction and destruction of the human form.

She knew it then, for the first time. She could do this job. It was a long way off, and medical school loomed on past college like a terrifying monster in her path, but if she could make it through all that . . . she could do this job. And be good at it.

"Thanks," she said to both doctors. "I needed something else to concentrate on."

"We all did," Dyson replied.

Slick seemed about to speak when there was a knock at the door. Dyson went to see who it was, and came back momentarily to announce that Dr. Martin, Agent Jeffries, and Detectives Gaines and Mariano were gathered upstairs.

"We're done here anyway," the M.E. announced. "Let's wash up and get on with it."

The first thing Jenna learned upon entering Slick's office was that her father was not going to die.

"Thanks to you, we really did get to him in time," Dr. Martin told her. "There's no trace of the disease in him at all."

Jenna whooped happily, hugged Dyson, and then gave the red-haired, elfin-looking CDC scientist a quick hug as well. Dr. Martin looked pretty uncomfortable with it, but that was her problem.

After that emotional outburst, it got pretty boring, as far as Jenna was concerned. It was mostly a rehash of the things they'd already discussed that morning, but this time, they were all awake. That, in itself, was a difference. Plus, the others had had a chance to get caught up with their respective bosses. The biggest surprise for Jenna had come before the meeting. She had expected that the others would consider her a "kid," and not bring her into the meeting. But Dyson had told her that Slick had insisted, saying that Jenna was part of his staff. She liked that.

Certainly they all knew it was only half true. But she was pleased to find that despite the questionable propriety of her presence, they all treated her like an adult. They all gave credence to what she had to say.

"Thanks for not treating me like a kid," she said when they were just about done.

It was Danny Mariano who laughed at that. "Jenna, come on," he said. "You had this whole thing figured out before any of us. I know I was guilty of thinking of you as, well, as a teenager, and I wasn't the only one. But you're in this thing now. Not to mention in danger."

That quieted the room. They all looked at Jenna and she felt very uncomfortable being studied so closely.

"Which brings us to our next topic," Detective Gaines said.

Jenna looked at her. Audrey was examining her closely. She seemed so stern, as usual, but then, suddenly, a kind smile spread across the detective's dark features.

"I'm sorry, Jenna, but you know you're a target."

"I hope you're not going to try to talk me into going home, too," Jenna said with a long sigh.

"No," Audrey replied. "But you can't stay in your dorm, either. Your father's in the hospital, so it's no problem to have a guard on him there. But you're another story. We've got to put you somewhere for a couple of nights."

"I could stay at my dad's," she suggested.

"First place he'd look," Agent Jeffries argued.

"Not necessarily," Slick countered. "As long as her father's in the hospital, the killer might not think of it. And for a night or two, until we figure something else out, or catch him, it's not a bad suggestion."

Jenna looked over at Danny. He was only Somerset Police, as opposed to Agent Jeffries, who was FBI. But she trusted him the most. There was something between them, somehow, and it wasn't anything romantic, either. Or at least, not much. She had the weird feeling that he understood her, especially after that first night at the campus police office.

"It'll work for now," Danny told her.

"Plus, we'll be watching you all the time," Detective Gaines added.

And she wasn't kidding.

For the next twenty-four hours, everywhere that Jenna went, the cops followed. Thursday morning, she turned around during her American Lit. class to see Danny Mariano sitting in the back. As handsome as he was, and as without-gray as his hair was, there was still no way he could pass for a student. A number of girls in class checked him out, and Jenna definitely noticed.

Later, walking across campus, she waited for him to catch up.

"Not very covert, us talking like this," he said as he approached her.

"That's all right," she told him. "Just thought I should thank you."

He smiled. "Not at all. I hope I'm not cramping your style."

It was Jenna's turn to smile. "Please. Like having a dashingly handsome older man following me across campus isn't good for my image? Trust me, I'll keep you around."

Danny actually blushed at that one, and Jenna laughed. She liked a man·who could blush.

She liked Danny.

Eighteen, meet thirtysomething, her mind warned, not for the first time. She laughed to herself and then walked on, leaving Danny to pick up her trail from afar again.

A killer involved in international political espionage wanted her dead, she had spent the previous afternoon pulling human organs out of a corpse, and she was falling for a cop thirteen years her senior.

I knew college was going to be interesting, Jenna thought. *But this is ridiculous.*

Later that night, she went over to the campus center with Hunter and Melody. Yoshiko was still at the dorm, feverishly working on a paper on the Industrial Revolution for her history class. Jenna had been tempted to stay in as well, just stay out of trouble, but that wouldn't have been fair to Melody.

Strange as it felt, they were celebrating.

"Can't lie to you, Mel," Jenna said, as she tossed her hair and then shrugged. "I'm jealous."

"Well, maybe it'll motivate you to actually audition next time," Melody replied, grinning.

She'd been cast in the coveted role of Maria in *The Sound of Music*. Hunter was going to play Rolf, which was a relatively small role, but came with one of the best songs in the show.

"At least I'll be there cheering you on," Jenna said. "I'll be like your groupie."

Hunter's eyes lit up. "I think I could get used to that idea."

Jenna scowled at him halfheartedly, and Melody gave him a light backhanded slap on the shoulder.

"Ow!" Hunter whined.

"Our mother raised us with better manners, sir," Melody said, allowing her Southern accent to deepen and become more pronounced.

"My apologies, ladies," Hunter replied, also laying the accent on thick. "I haven't behaved as a proper gentleman, to my deep and abiding shame."

They both laughed, and Jenna sighed. "I know you guys probably think I'm a total goof, but I just love it when you talk like that. The whole *Gone With the Wind* thing is so romantic."

"Oh, yeah," Melody replied, her voice back to normal. "The Old South just sparkled with romance, if you take out slavery and the Civil War."

"You know what I mean, LaChance," Jenna said, glaring at Melody.

"Sure she does," Hunter agreed, "but we both like the look you get on your face when someone teases you."

Jenna glared at them both, then. Hunter and Melody laughed, and she couldn't help smiling. Jenna knew their going out tonight hadn't been just to celebrate the casting of the show, but also to distract her from what was going on in her life.

She was in danger. Which meant they might be putting themselves in danger as well, just being there with her. She was surprised, in some ways, that they were willing to even hang out with her. But she was also glad.

Besides, the cops were keeping an eye on her. She ought to be safe. Although, whoever had taken over for Danny at the end of the day, she hadn't spotted them. Obviously, her current shadow was better at blending into the college crowd.

Either that, or they'd stopped surveillance on her for the moment. She didn't like *that* idea at all.

Late that night, Jenna sat in her father's second-floor apartment and sipped tea. She had tried several times to go to sleep, and been unable to do more than close her eyes. Eventually, she'd surrendered, and gotten up from bed. Nothing on television interested her, but she had to do something to distract her mind, make her forget she had insomnia.

She found her way to her father's desk and booted up his computer. There, in a folder very clearly marked "Gutierrez," were all the research materials originally collected by Professor Mattei, as well as her father's presentation in progress. The very information that had gotten them all into this trouble to begin with. It made her feel a little ill, seeing it all there. But then she opened up the file with the report that her father was finishing for his dead friend, and she started to read.

Carlos Gutierrez, the man who wanted to rule Costa Rica, was a savage beast of a man, a vicious tyrant and a killer, a man who sold drugs to children around the world, and did it with a song in his heart and a spring in his step. It was hard for Jenna to imagine that her life, and her father's life, were in jeopardy because of a brutal man half a world away. Even harder to connect the violence and death she'd witnessed firsthand to that man.

But as she read through that file, it became a little easier.

And she grew to hate Carlos Gutierrez.

After a time, she found her eyes closing. She stretched and yawned and closed the file, shut down the computer, and then rose from her father's desk. With the fog of sleep starting to engulf her, she walked slowly back to the bedroom, slipped under the covers, and closed her eyes.

Drifting off . . . fog . . . smoke . . .

Then her eyes snapped open.

She sniffed the air, and smelled smoke. Heart racing wildly, Jenna leaped from the bed and ran to the door that led to the stairwell. Without a thought, she yanked it open.

The wall opposite the door was on fire, and flames were licking across the ceiling and the landing in front of her as well. Behind her, the smoke detector in her father's living room began to buzz angrily, joining the chorus of smoke detectors coming up from downstairs.

From below, a man's voice, a familiar voice, shouted: "Get back in there, you bitch!"

Then Shayna Emerson screamed.

c h a p t e r 1 3

The house was on fire. Smoke was starting to fill the place, and Jenna narrowed her eyes and held her breath. She'd heard that one scream from downstairs—from Shayna—and then nothing more. Now she started down, moving as best she could.

Please God, don't let her be dead, she thought to herself. And then, gravely, *I wish I'd never gotten involved with this. Any of it.*

It was the fear talking, and she knew that. But that didn't make it any easier. For Jenna was afraid, no doubt. Profoundly afraid. But she was also furious at the people who were willing to kill her, and her father, and anyone else connected with Professor Mattei's papers on Costa Rican politics, just to keep playing a game of drugs and power that should have been stopped a long time ago.

With a whoosh of crackling air, fire spread up the banister to her right, as though it had been doused in oil. Jenna screamed, and then sucked in nothing but superheated smoke.

She choked, began to cough, sucking in more smoke, and she nearly stumbled and fell as she moved down the stairs. But she didn't dare. She couldn't allow herself to fall. The stairs themselves were starting to burn now. The walls were burning on either side of her. Her eyes were watering from the smoke. She bit her lip.

I don't want to die! her mind screamed, and she tried desperately to stay calm, though her heart kept pumping faster and she felt as though she couldn't breathe. She felt woozy, disoriented. Too much smoke inhalation.

Then she was only a few steps from the first-floor landing. Around the corner and down a short hall was the door to Shayna Emerson's apartment. Shayna had screamed, and Jenna knew she had to help. But straight ahead was the front door, and God help her, Jenna knew she wanted desperately to get out that door. At the moment, it was much more important than Shayna's scream. *I have to . . .*

"No!" she snapped aloud, cursing herself, and the fire, as she burst into another fit of coughing.

She could barely stand as she reached the bottom of the stairs. The door to Shayna's apartment was set back into a short hall next to the stairs. Jenna turned into the hallway, and then she only stood and stared, eyes wide. The door to Shayna's apartment was open wide. Inside, Jenna could see that some of the furniture was on fire, the beautiful floor-length Victorian drapes were blazing. Even the ceiling was burning. There were smoke detectors still buzzing, but one of them was blackened and melted on the ceiling.

But Shayna wasn't inside. The pale, black-haired, rather gothic-looking English professor lay crumpled on the floor in the hallway, bleeding from a gash on her forehead. The walls around her were blackening as the flames licked across them.

The floor was steaming.

The whole place was filling with smoke, and Jenna was feeling even shakier on her feet than before. She tried to cover her mouth, breathe through her cupped hand. It didn't help.

"Shayna!" she said, coughing again as she fell to her knees next to the woman's still form.

She felt for a pulse, found it, and figured that was reassurance enough. She wished she knew a little bit more about real medicine and first aid and all of that . . . but such thoughts would have to wait.

Then, as though it had been lying in wait for her like some jungle animal, the fire erupted around her. The floor began to burn and Shayna's robe was suddenly alight.

For only a moment, Jenna thought about picking her up. Instantly, she realized how ridiculous that was. She was strong; she might be able to drag Shayna. But Jenna couldn't carry the woman, certainly not while she could barely breathe.

The door!

Jenna cursed herself for her stupidity as she turned and ran for the front door of the house.

She stuck her hand inside her shirt and reached out to unlock the dead bolt. But the door was already unlocked! *Of course it is,* she snapped at herself. Whoever had been in here, whoever had attacked Shayna, had left it unlocked on their way out.

She grabbed the knob. Even through the cotton, it was hot enough to burn her. She cried out as she turned and pulled.

The door didn't budge. She pulled again; still nothing.

In Shayna's apartment, the ceiling caved in with an explosion of flame and rushing oxygen that only fed the blaze.

Jenna screamed, and then collapsed in a fit of coughing and hacking. She glanced over at Shayna, and saw that the woman's robe was really burning now. She was probably being burned.

Shayna was going to die if she didn't do something.

Hell, I'm going to die! she thought, completely panicked.

Something banged against the door.

Jenna looked up, wide-eyed. Then she cried out again, as loud as she could.

"Help!" She choked back more smoke. "Help us, please!"

"Jenna! Back off!" said a voice beyond the door.

She scrambled back into the hallway as best she could. Ignoring the door a moment, she went to Shayna's side, grabbed the part of her robe that wasn't on fire, and pulled it away and off her. The fire gobbled it up in an instant.

The door shook from an impact. Then another.

Then it burst open, the frame shattering in a spray of fire and burnt wood.

"Danny!" Jenna choked out.

He rushed into the burning house, eyes wide and anxious. In a heartbeat, he was by her side.

"Go!" he told her. "I'll get the professor."

Jenna did as she was told. She stumbled out the door and onto the front lawn of the burning building. She collapsed on the grass, then turned over onto her back to see Detective Mariano coming down the steps with Shayna slung over his shoulder. Her nightgown was singed and her left arm looked red and raw where it had been burned.

But Jenna thought she was alive.

Alive is good.

Jenna choked and sucked in fresh air. Her eyelids fluttered and she started to lose consciousness. What seemed like a moment later, but might have been much more than that, she began to come around again. She could hear sirens, and that was good, too. The house was probably a lost cause, but at least the other houses on the block could be saved from the blaze. Not her father's house, though.

She swallowed. The heated smoke had burned her throat, and it was a painful movement. But she realized something else. All the paperwork—Professor Mattei's work, the material her father had been collating, all the evidence against Carlos Gutierrez—it was all gone, now. The fire would consume it all.

The fire trucks had started to arrive. The hydrants

were opened, and water began splashing the blaze at high power.

"Hey, kid, you okay?"

Jenna looked up at the voice and saw Audrey Gaines staring down at her, concern on the cop's normally stern face.

"I will be," she said. "Thanks to Danny."

"Yeah," Audrey said, a half smile on her lips. "He's a regular hero. And a heartbreaker to boot."

Huh? Jenna looked more closely at her, wondering if Audrey was just talking about Danny's looks, or if there was more to her words than that. Maybe she'd noticed that Jenna had a little crush on her partner. Not that it mattered right now. *Or ever, for that matter.*

"It's all gone," Jenna said. "All the documentation about Gutierrez."

Then, suddenly, Danny was there as well. He came over beside Audrey and kneeled down next to Jenna.

"Yeah, we figure that's why the fire," Danny said. "Guy probably didn't even know you were in there."

"We don't know that," Audrey warned.

"You're right," Danny agreed. "Best to be careful, of course. But I think once he knew he'd screwed up trying to kill both you and your dad, he just wanted the information gone. And maybe it was partially a warning, too."

"Maybe they won't come after my dad and me again if we keep our mouths shut, you mean?" Jenna asked, staring at the two state police detectives.

"Maybe," Audrey agreed.

"Like hell," Jenna said angrily, and coughed painfully again. "What happened, anyway? I mean, nobody saw the guy? Nobody noticed the house was on fire?"

Danny glanced away, shifting uncomfortably.

"We had a pair of screwups on duty tonight. Jacobs and Curran. This kind of thing isn't their usual detail," Audrey told her.

"Are they blind?" Jenna asked, coughing again.

"They went to get coffee," Danny told her, looking furious. "Audrey and I were coming to relieve them when we saw the flames."

Jenna stared at him, horrified. "So, thanks to the lure of Starbucks, I'd be dead now, except that you guys happened to show up at just the right time?"

"That's about it," Audrey agreed.

"I think I may be sick," Jenna muttered.

But, though she did feel slightly nauseous, she didn't get sick. Instead, she sat up, tried to get to her feet, and got a bit woozy again. She looked over at the intersection and saw a bunch of students, and some professors as well, had come out of the dorms and houses in their sweats and robes in the wee small hours of the morning to watch as two paramedics loaded the still unconscious Shayna Emerson into an ambulance.

Jenna took several deep breaths, and started to try to stand again. Danny put a hand on her shoulder to keep her there.

"Hey," he said. "Relax a minute. Too much smoke."

Then the paramedics were there, hovering around Jenna, taking her vital signs. They helped her up and asked if she wanted to go over to the medical center in an ambulance, which she declined.

"I'll take you," Danny said quickly. "You have to get a doc to check you out, and there's no way you're going alone. We have to figure out what's happening here."

Jenna looked over at Audrey and raised her eyebrows. Detective Gaines was the senior of the two, and Jenna thought that, bright as Danny was, Audrey was the more seasoned as well.

"Better safe," Audrey said simply.

"Than sorry," Jenna agreed, nodding. "All right, let's go."

Danny put his arm around Jenna's waist and helped her move down the street, past the police cordon, to his car. She felt him there, close to her, so strong and alive, and she remembered the way he'd looked as he came through the door of the burning house to save her.

And maybe she leaned on him a little bit more than she had to.

Once they were in the car, and moving, Danny spoke up. "Why don't you tell me about it."

Jenna looked at him. His eyes were on the road, but for just a moment, his gaze wavered and he glanced at her, obviously concerned.

"I guess you'll want a statement anyway, right?" she asked.

"Eventually," he agreed. "Right now, I'm just trying to figure out what happened. A lot of things don't make sense."

Jenna frowned at that. She took a breath, swallowed and still found it difficult, but not quite as painful. Her chest hurt.

"I don't know, it all seems to make sense to me," she said. "A horrible, vicious kind of sense, but it's not like I don't get it."

Danny actually smiled, chuckled a little. "All right, Sherlock. Enlighten me."

Jenna stared out at the streetlights. They had to go the long way around the campus to avoid all the emergency vehicles, but they were coming up on Somerset Medical Center now.

"I heard a man," she said, speaking to the window, to the night beyond, and to the reflection of Danny behind the wheel. "I knew the voice, too. The same guy who came after me that night. He yelled something like 'Get in there, bitch,' or whatever. Then Shayna . . . Professor Emerson . . . screamed.

"The way I figure it, she may have been up already, or the son of a bitch woke her up while he was splashing gas or whatever he used to set the fire. Doesn't matter. She was awake. The fire started to spread, the smoke was all over the place. She went to the door. He backed her into the hallway and knocked her out. Then he jammed the door with something from outside, to keep her inside if she came around, and me, too—if he knew I was there. And then he took off. By that time, the fire was already cooking along real nice."

Jenna choked out a short, painful laugh.

"Maybe he forgot his marshmallows."

Danny nodded thoughtfully. "That all fits," he agreed.

"Glad you think so," Jenna replied. "Question is, what do we do now?"

Danny steered the car into the emergency room parking lot and slid it into an empty space.

"Detective Gaines is going to question Professor Emerson as soon as she comes around. We need a description of this guy, Jenna. That'll be a breakthrough for us, if we can get it."

Jenna waited for more, but there wasn't any. She felt a little sick. She wanted to yell at him. "That's all?" she wanted to scream. "That's the best you can do, business as usual?"

But it won't do any good.

"What time is it?" she asked as they climbed out of the car.

Danny looked at his watch. "Quarter past one."

Jenna sighed. Too late to call Melody. She'd have to call her first thing in the morning. And Yoshiko, too. She needed her friends around her now. Needed to talk to someone who would understand her fear without drawing attention to it. And then there were her parents. Jenna wanted to talk to them, felt the need to be comforted by both her mother and her father, but she knew that this would only add to their concerns about her job.

At the automatic doors to the ER, she stopped

Danny with a hand on his arm. He looked at her, alarmed.

"Do you need help?" he asked quickly.

"No," she said, shaking her head, smiling shyly. "I just . . . I wanted to thank you for saving my life."

The detective looked uncomfortable for a moment. Then he smiled back, a bit flustered. "Don't mention it."

Jenna grinned. "Okay."

Then she led the way into the ER, and hoped the doctors could do something to soothe her throat, and get the coughing to stop.

"You can go home," Dr. Heckler said, shaking her head. "The last thing we need is two Logans in one hospital."

Jenna blinked a moment before she understood. "It's Blake, actually. Logan is my dad's name."

Her voice wasn't much more than a whisper, now. The doctor had given her something for the pain, but it was still uncomfortable to swallow and to talk, and she'd found it less so if she whispered instead.

"Oh," Dr. Heckler said, blinking. "Sorry, I didn't realize—"

"No problem," Jenna told her. "It's a common mistake. So I can go home now?"

"As far as I'm concerned you can," the woman replied. "The police may have other ideas, however. Detective Mariano is hovering about out in chairs . . . I mean, in the waiting room."

Jenna nodded, happy to have had some of the pure

oxygen the hospital had given her through a funky plastic mask. "Great. I appreciate it, Doc. I was glad to see you here. And thanks for not calling Dr. Slikowski."

Dr. Heckler was cleaning up the exam room. As Jenna stood, the doctor slipped her white lab coat back on. She looked over at Jenna kindly.

"You work for him, and he's a part of this whole crazy mess," Dr. Heckler said. "I just wasn't sure if you'd want me to call."

"I understand. But why wake him up tonight? It'll be dawn in a few hours. Nothing else is going to happen between now and then."

Out in the waiting room, Danny looked up and smiled when Jenna emerged from the ER.

"So you're all right?" he asked.

Jenna brushed her hair away from her eyes. "Clean bill of health," she confirmed in a whisper. "The doc said I could go home."

"Back to the dorm, you mean?" Danny asked uncertainly. "I don't know if I like that idea. If this guy is still after you, and we have to assume that's the case, the dorm is going to be his next stop. I've already talked to my lieutenant, and he agrees that we ought to put you up in a hotel for the night."

Anxiety roiled in Jenna's gut. She was running. The idea didn't sit well with her. But neither did the idea of getting killed for her pride and stubbornness.

"Can I get room service?" she croaked.

Danny smiled. "Sure. Just don't order champagne or anything."

"Wouldn't dream of it," Jenna promised. "Let me just look in on my father first, all right?"

"Fine. He's got a guard on him anyway, so you should be all right. I'm going to check in with Audrey. She's upstairs with Professor Emerson—who's going to be fine, by the way. Second-degree burns on her arm and a mild concussion. Not bad. I want to see if we've got anything yet on our firebug.

"I'll meet you back down here in ten minutes."

When she stepped off the elevator, Jenna walked slowly down the corridor, taking long, gentle breaths. Her chest was still tight and the cough had not gone away entirely, but she was all right. *I'm gonna be all right.*

It all came crashing down on to her with great suddenness. Twice, someone had attempted to take her life. This time, he had almost succeeded. Jenna paused and covered her eyes with her right hand.

"Don't get all freaky now, Blake," she croaked to herself.

"Can I help you, young lady?"

Jenna looked up quickly. A few feet away, a diminutive woman in nurse's whites stared at her.

"I just . . . I wanted to see my father. Frank Logan?"

"It's two o'clock in the morning," the nurse said, frowning at her. "It's long past visiting hours, dear."

"I know," Jenna said quickly. The woman must have thought she was an idiot. "Look, I was just in for treatment myself. I was in a fire tonight. And my dad is . . ."

Jenna frowned. Down the hall, the door to her father's hospital room, 655K, was half open. Inside, the light was on. There was no guard in sight. *Probably someone else who needed a cup of coffee.*

For a moment, she froze. "Oh, Dad, no," she whispered.

Then, fear rushing through her, she pushed past the nurse, who protested only a moment before also noticing the light on. The woman sighed in frustration and went after Jenna, urging her to be quiet so as not to wake the other patients.

Jenna barely heard her. "Call security," she told the woman. "Get the police!"

She ran the last few feet, not stopping to give a moment's thought to her own life. The only thing that mattered in those few seconds was preventing her father's death. She slammed her shoulder into the door and it banged open.

"Get away from him, you son of a . . ."

Jenna's voice trailed off.

Standing next to the bed where Frank Logan lay sleeping, Agent Jeffries looked up at her in surprise. Then a friendly smile spread across his face and he let out a breath.

"Jenna," he said. "You startled me. Audrey Gaines called me about the fire. I thought I'd look in on your father.

"I'm glad you're all right."

"What's going on here?" the nurse behind her demanded.

Jeffries's smile was warm and comforting. But there was something different in his voice, something she'd never heard there before.

And then she knew she was wrong.

She had heard it before, just never made the connection.

Jenna's eyes went wide. She knew that voice.

"You," she croaked.

The smile disappeared from his face. His eyes darted to the left, and Jenna followed his gaze. In a darkened corner of the room, a pair of legs in pressed policeman's blue poked out from behind a chair.

The guard.

"Oh God," Jenna whisperd.

Jeffries reached into his jacket and pulled out a gun.

chapter 14

It all seemed to happen in a single instant. Agent Jeffries drew his gun, aware now that Jenna had recognized his voice and had seen the corpse of the policeman who'd been guarding her father in the corner of the room. Her father's eyes flickered open at the sound of her own voice. The nurse who had tried to stop her from going in to see her father began to shout loudly as soon as she saw Jeffries standing there in the dimly lit room.

"You there!" the nurse snapped. "What are you doing in here? Like I just told this girl, visiting . . ."

The nurse went on like that as she pushed past Jenna into the room. It was almost as though she didn't even notice Jeffries pulling his gun. Then, suddenly, she froze, right in front of Jenna.

"Oh, God, what are you—" she managed to squeak out.

Then Jeffries shot her in the head.

The gun made a muffled thump through its silencer. In his hospital bed, Frank Logan was wide awake now. He sat up in an instant and lunged toward the killer even before the bossy nurse's corpse hit the floor.

"Jenna, run!" her father roared.

For just a moment, she couldn't move. She was looking at the nurse and wondering if she'd be weighing the woman's organs the next afternoon. Then there came that muffled thump again, and a bullet punched into the wall behind Jenna's head. She looked up to see her father struggling with Jeffries.

"Run!" Jenna's father shouted again.

Jeffries turned and batted him hard across the face with the knuckles of his left hand. Jenna saw her father go down, and Jeffries turned toward her.

She ran.

Her father had commanded her to do so. And she knew that if she ran, Jeffries would come after her. He had to come after her. There wasn't anything she could do, physically, to protect her father. But if she ran, she might draw the killer away. She could use herself as bait.

With a shriek that she cursed herself for, Jenna sprinted into the corridor and down the hall toward the door to the stairwell. The elevators would have taken too long. Jeffries would be right on her heels.

But he wasn't. Jenna glanced over her shoulder when she was nearly to the stairwell door.

There was shouting from down the corridor. Nurses or orderlies, someone running. But even amidst that noise, Jenna heard a sound that froze her heart. The muffled pop of a silenced gun.

"Daddy, no!" she screamed, and started back for his room.

Which was when Jeffries stepped out into the hallway, smiling at her. He held the gun in both hands, aimed at her. He was FBI, or had been before he'd sold himself out to the highest bidder. He was trained with a gun. She was dead.

"Hey, buddy! What the hell are you doing up here?" shouted a burly orderly as he came around the nurses' station and reached for Jeffries from behind.

Cursing loudly, Jeffries turned and shot the man.

Jenna spun and slammed through the door to the stairwell. The heavy metal door banged against concrete, and then started to close. Jenna took off down the stairs. She hurried down half a dozen, and then jumped the rest of the way to the landing between the two, slamming against the cement wall. Just as she launched herself down toward the fifth floor, the door above banged open again, and Jeffries roared at her.

"Damn you, little girl, come back here! You know you're not going to get away from me again. You were lucky the first time."

Jenna didn't reply. She pounded down five steps this time, and then jumped for the fifth-floor landing. While she was going down toward the fourth-floor landing, Jeffries was nearly an entire flight of stairs behind. She was putting more distance between them, moving slightly faster than he was.

At any floor, she could have stopped. Could have pushed through a door and into a corridor that was working on half-light, with a graveyard shift staff and sleeping patients. She might be able to escape him, then.

But escape wasn't enough for her. This man had just killed two nurses, and likely her father as well. With the image of her father, shot, burning in her brain, and her heart and lungs working overtime as she struggled to focus on running . . . on not falling . . . Jenna had made a decision.

No stopping.

Not until she reached the first floor. Because on the first floor, in the lobby, Danny Mariano was waiting for her. Danny Mariano, who was a cop. Danny Mariano, who carried a gun.

Above her, Jeffries, the killer, began to shout again. "It's all over for me now, don't you get it, Jenna? I'm done here. I've got nothing to lose. When this is all over, I walk out of here and disappear into Central America and nobody will even bother to look far enough to find me.

"You're dead, girl," he huffed. "Accept it. Hell, I was gonna do you quick, but now you're just pissing me off. That's the number one rule, Jenna. Don't piss me off. But you've gone and done it now. I'm going to kill you.

"And I'm going to make it hurt."

Jenna blocked him out, forced herself not even to listen to the words. She ran down steps, and jumped, her fingers sliding along metal railings. She hit the landings, bounced off walls, and just kept going.

And before she knew it, she'd reached the first floor. There was a big "1" painted on the wall next to the door. Unlike the others, all of which opened out into the stairwell, this door was larger, more elaborate, and it opened into the hospital instead. There was a small window in it as well, but it was high on the door and webbed with wire mesh, and she couldn't see anyone beyond. She had nearly a flight and a half lead now, but even as she paused, catching her breath, to go for the door, Jeffries was catching up.

Jenna slammed the metal bar at the middle of the door, and it gave. The door started to open, and then slammed into something with a clang of metal. It opened only three inches or so. Not nearly enough for Jenna to slip through. She slammed her body against it, and it moved another two inches. Then she saw what it was. A gurney, brakes locked, blocked the door.

Some idiot had blocked the door!

With a few more shoves, she'd be through. Then she'd get to Danny, and Danny would . . .

But she didn't have time for a few more shoves. She heard the heavy breathing of the killer and the pounding of his feet on the stairs. She looked up and saw his shadow on the wall.

He was about to hit the landing just above, to round the corner where he'd see her. Where he'd be in range to shoot her.

Jenna cursed, and she turned and ran for the stairs. Down. Down, down, and down.

She hadn't been frightened before, not really. It was a form of terror, but it had been channeled through her into her hatred and anger and her need to hurt this man so desperately.

But now . . . she wouldn't be seeing Danny. She could have left the stairs on any floor, but now she was headed for the basement.

"I see you!" he screamed.

Jenna was about to deny it, to yell back that he could not see her, when a bullet dug a chunk out of the cement just behind her head. She didn't look up, but she knew instantly that he must have hung over the railing to get a shot at her. An impossible shot, but he'd taken it anyway. He didn't care how she died; he just wanted to be sure he killed her.

And he was close.

"Ohgodohgodplease!" Jenna muttered to herself.

Her chest felt as though it would explode, and her head hurt. She tasted salty tears and realized that she had begun to cry and been unaware of it. Now she forced herself to stop. She bit her lip and would not cry anymore. Not because of him. He'd harmed her enough already. Thanks to him, she'd had to see her professor, and her father's closest friend, commit murder and then drop dead before her eyes. She'd been attacked, and her father had nearly been killed . . . and might even now be lying dead upstairs.

He was just a hired gun. Jenna knew that. He worked for Carlos Gutierrez, who had likely ordered it all. But none of that mattered. Gutierrez wasn't here. Jeffries, on the other hand, was. His hands had done the deeds. He'd betrayed his duty as a federal agent, and he seemed to rejoice in the fact that he'd become little more than a killer for hire.

Jenna despised him.

She was terrified of him.

For a moment, as she reached the basement, with him so close behind, she had the horrible thought that the door might be locked. This late at night, the morgue itself was locked up and the attendant worked in a small office down the hall. He'd have the key. But she didn't know if the door was locked, and in that heartbeat, she was terrified that it would be.

They won't have very far to move my body if he catches up with me.

She grabbed the metal bar and pulled. The door swung in easily just as Jeffries hit the landing above. A bullet pinged against the metal, piercing one side of the door and lodging in it. The man cursed loudly.

Then Jenna was off again. But now he was close behind. Too close. Most of the doors down here would be locked, and if she just ran straight down the corridor toward the elevators, he'd have her in his sights the moment he exited the stairwell.

She had one choice.

The door to the autopsy room was nine feet away. She ran for it, twisted the knob, and pushed into the room only seconds before Jeffries came through the stairwell door into the hall. She had no idea if he'd seen her enter, or seen the door click shut.

In the darkness, she wanted to scream in terror.

But she was trapped in here now, with nowhere else to go. If she screamed, she'd be dead for sure.

"Damn it!" Danny snapped.

He stared at the still, bleeding form of Frank Logan, and cursed himself for not being here. He should have known they would have tried to kill the man while he was in the hospital. But they'd all been so cocky, so arrogant. The killer had taken his shot at Frank and failed, so they'd all concentrated on Jenna. It had been foolish.

And Frank had paid for it.

Not with his life, thank God, Danny thought. He'd taken a bullet in the shoulder. But he'd live. More than Danny could say of the two nurses that lay dead on the sixth floor.

They'd been careless. Now Jenna might have to pay for it, too.

"Frank!" Danny said, snapping his fingers in front of the man's face.

"Back off, Detective. We've got to take care of this wound," declared a doctor who was a little too bossy for Danny's tastes.

Danny shoved him out of the way. He snapped his fingers in front of Frank's face again.

"Logan, come on! Where's Jenna? Where'd she go?"

The professor's eyes fluttered open. He focused enough to see that it was Danny's face above him.

"Stairs," he croaked.

Then his eyes closed again, and he continued to

bleed. The doctor started to say something snide to Danny, but the detective ignored him. He was already on his way out the door, shouldering through hospital personnel. He glanced up toward the elevators, then back down the hall toward the stairs.

"Hang on, kid," he muttered to himself, trying to convince himself that Jenna was still alive.

Danny drew his service weapon, and hit the stairs at a run. An image of Jenna filled his head, her piercing eyes, her smart-aleck attitude. Gun at the ready, he slammed through the door, fearing that at any turn, he might come upon Jenna's still warm corpse, lying on the stairs.

Grimly, Danny started down.

In the darkened autopsy room, Jenna crouched behind the huge metal table and tried desperately to think. It wouldn't take long for Jeffries to figure out what room she was hiding in. The dark would give her a slight advantage—she knew the terrain in here, every cable and contraption, and he didn't—but that wouldn't be much. And she couldn't stop him from turning on the lights, after all.

Stupid. She didn't have a chance in hell. Nobody was coming down here, not this late. Not unless she got ridiculously lucky, and someone was wheeling a corpse to the morgue right about the time she started screaming for her life.

Great. A lot to hope for.

Her mind felt like it had slowed, or frozen. *Yeah, frozen's more like it,* she thought. Then it hit her. Frozen. The autopsy room had its own fridge. It was never used to store bodies for lengthy periods, only briefly before an autopsy, or if there was a break in the proceedings. Because of that, the temperature was just about fifty degrees.

But Jeffries probably didn't know that. He might not expect her to hide in what he'd assume was a refrigerator. He might not . . . or he might. It wasn't like she had much choice now. She had to go somewhere, and there wasn't any back door.

If she was lucky, he'd peek in, and then move on down the hall. Maybe he'd actually leave if she could keep him guessing long enough. After all, the nurse upstairs would be discovered eventually. And . . . and her father. He couldn't afford to wait too long.

Neither can you! Jenna cursed herself.

Quietly as she could, she slid open a metal drawer from the counter behind her, and reached her fingers in. She went as slowly as she was able, afraid to cut herself, and eventually picked up a scalpel without slicing her fingers to ribbons.

Feeling her way in the darkness, Jenna went to the "cold room," as Slick called it. Dyson usually preferred the term "icebox," which Jenna thought was a bit cruder, but always made her smile. She wished Dyson were here now. She wished anyone were here now, in fact.

Anyone who wasn't trying to kill her, anyway.

The icebox door clicked as she pulled it closed behind her, and she had a moment of fear wondering if she'd be able to open it again from the inside. But it was an irrational fear. She knew the door could open from inside. That sort of thing—someone trapped inside a refrigerated room with a dead man—only happened on bad television series. Plus, there was no dead guy in here.

There better not be. She felt around in the dark, fingers touching the metal bars of a gurney. Tentatively, she moved her hand over its surface, but it was unoccupied.

Nodding to herself, she slid behind the gurney, crouched there, holding the scalpel tightly in her right hand. She had no sooner gotten into that position than she heard the sound of the door to the autopsy room closing.

Jenna stopped breathing.

He was here. In the room. Just beyond the door. No light came around the edges of the door, but she knew he would have turned the light on. He knew that this was where she worked—knew far too much about her. Yeah, he'd have turned the lights on, and come into the room . . . she couldn't hear anything at the moment. No footsteps, no thumps or crashing as he checked behind the table or pushed over the camera array.

Which was how she knew. The killer didn't *think* she was here. He knew it. He'd come in, flicked on the lights . . .

. . . and seen the metal drawer slid wide open, the drawer out of which she'd taken the scalpel. He knew she was here, and knew that she was armed. Even now, he'd have taken a good look at the room, and he would have figured it all out.

He had to know right where she was hiding.

So she crouched there, in the cold, dark room, and her heart seemed to seize up in her chest. She bit her lip and vowed to herself that she would not cry. That she would not give him that satisfaction. Jenna promised herself that if she was going to die, she would hurt him first. Make it *cost* him something.

And she knew in her heart that it was all crap. That she was an eighteen-year-old girl with no fighting experience against a man whose life was apparently full of murder. That in all likelihood she would never see her mother again, or Melody or Yoshiko or any of her friends from home. She'd never know if her father was alive or dead.

"But I'll be with you, Daddy," she whispered, so quietly not even this tiny room allowed an echo.

A tear formed at the corner of her left eye, and she was enraged by it. A promise she'd made to herself only eyeblinks before, now broken. All because of him. This man. This killer who had violated her life in every way imaginable.

The autopsy room, beyond the little door, was completely silent. Jenna bit her lip to keep from screaming out her fear and rage and sorrow. She hung her head and her shoulders began to quiver.

And the door to the cold room opened.

Agent Jeffries was silhouetted in the light streaming in from the autopsy room. Jenna looked up, and her eyes met those of the killer, the man who wanted to take her life.

"Damn you!" she screamed, her throat raw with the emotion and fury of it.

As she screamed, she put all her weight into pushing the gurney, bent low, head down. There was a dull pop as Jeffries fired once before the gurney slammed painfully into his upper thighs. The man was thrown off balance by the impact, thrust backward, stumbling, falling back into the autopsy room.

He was down. Trying to stand. Bringing his gun up again. Jenna was overcome by her fear and rage. Her eyes were dry now, her adrenaline rushing through every cell, urging her on. She shoved the gurney aside and lunged for him, brought the scalpel down with her right hand. Jeffries lifted his left arm to block, and the blade sank deep into his forearm, scraping bone.

Then he hit her across the face with his gun. The cold metal split her skin over her cheekbone and her blood spattered his clothes and hair, and she was down.

And she was dead. She knew that, just as surely as she knew her own name. Jeffries was glaring at her now, his silence horrible. He stared down at the scalpel still jutting out of his left arm as he rose up to his knees. Shakily, he pointed the silenced barrel of his gun at her face, where she lay on her back.

"What a pity," he snarled. "You won't even be pretty anymore."

Jenna's brain screamed at her body to move, to get

out of the way. But even if it weren't for the blazing pain of her battered face, or the numbness she felt creeping over her brain from the shock of the attack, she knew she couldn't outrace a bullet. She knew that.

She didn't move.

The door to the autopsy room slammed open. Danny Mariano stood there with both hands on his weapon, ready to fire. And if Jenna hadn't knocked the killer down, it might have ended right there. Danny would have had the drop on him.

But Jeffries was on his knees. The second the door burst in, he fell backward, aiming his weapon at the figure in the open doorway, and squeezed off a shot. A huge sliver was torn out of the door frame as Danny ducked away, cursing loudly.

"Jenna!" he called.

She didn't respond. It was a standoff, now. Gun for gun. And she would be a hostage soon, no doubt. But Jenna didn't want to be a hostage.

With all the strength she could muster, Jenna planted her feet on the cold tile floor, and shoved, sliding backward over the smooth surface. Jeffries started to turn back toward her, but Danny popped his head around the corner again, and the killer took another shot at the detective.

By then, Jenna was up. Reaching for a rack of tools above the autopsy table. Her fingers closed around a familiar object, something she'd seen used many times before, but never laid hands on herself. Until now.

A long black cable trailed from it. Jenna stumbled toward Jeffries. The killer began to turn toward her, either sensing her approach or ready to use her as a human shield. It didn't matter. For in that moment, Jenna turned it *on*. The gun started to come up, but too late. The spinning, razor-sharp end of the bone saw tore into the killer's face and he screamed as though he were being gutted.

He tried, with his wounded hand, to reach for the saw. With his right hand, he raised the gun and shot again. But too soon. The bullet went wild.

Jenna fell to the ground, cradling her bleeding face and waiting to die.

"Drop it!" Danny shouted from the doorway.

Jeffries raised his gun again, trying to turn toward Danny.

The detective fired twice. Jenna was wiping his blood, mingled with her own, from her face, as Jeffries fell down on top of her. Jenna screamed and wiggled out from beneath Jeffries's body, even as the man's lifeblood spread across the cold tile.

Then Danny was there, reaching for her, helping her up. He pulled her into his arms, and held her there for a long while.

She let him.

epilogue

Several nights later, Jenna sat inside the House of Blues in Harvard Square, listening to Keb' Mo' play a soulful set, and eating a fiery jambalaya that was making Hunter's eyes water just smelling it. Melody and Yoshiko were there as well.

"Thanks, guys," she said, looking around the darkened blues club, a smile on her face. A smile that caused her a little bit of pain, given the stitches.

"Please," Yoshiko said, rolling her eyes. "If *I'm* sick of your mom hanging around, and visiting your dad in the hospital, I can't even imagine how *you* must feel."

Jenna laughed, nodding. "I know," she agreed. "Good old April's been a little bit of a nudge. I'll have to remind her that I'm the one going to college here, not her."

"She means well," Melody reminded them all. "She's your mom, after all. She's supposed to go a little nuts if somebody tries to kill you."

"I'll remember that," Jenna said.

It was a night she had sorely needed, and she was more grateful than she could ever put into words. She'd been in e-mail contact with some of her high school friends, including both Moira and Priya, but somehow, she took no comfort in their concern. They weren't here. They weren't in it with her. Melody and Yoshiko and Hunter were. It was as though, somehow, the friends that she'd had when she was a kid would always be a part of that—her childhood.

This was different.

Of course, I'd never thought of attempted murder as a rite of passage. But then, she'd always moved to the beat of a different drum, so to speak.

"How is your father, anyway?" Melody asked.

Jenna shrugged a little. "He's cranky," she said. "But he'll be all right. The bullet didn't break any bones and didn't do much muscle damage, either. If being poisoned with a biological weapon and then being shot can be called lucky, I'd guess he's it."

"Y'all are both lucky," Melody reminded her.

"Oh, right," Yoshiko agreed, shaking her head. "We should all be that lucky."

"You really know how to make a girl feel better," Jenna said, frowning sternly. But only for a moment.

"Did your dad talk to that guy from the State Department today?" Yoshiko asked.

Jenna nodded. "With what they already knew, and my father's statements, nobody'll be able to deny what Gutierrez is really up to. Actually, from what my dad says, just what's already been reported in the media here has started a big backlash against him in Costa Rica.

"He's done."

She paused a moment, looking at her friends.

"I really want to thank you guys," Jenna said. "I don't think I'd have gotten through this if you hadn't been here. I'd probably have gone home, just like my mother wanted me to."

"Yeah, but what would the death docs do without ya?" Hunter asked.

The girls all raised their eyebrows and stared at him. Hunter ignored them. He was getting used to being ganged up on. Which only made them do it all the more.

"So, what did the doctors say about your face?" he asked, pressing onward.

"Hunter LaChance!" Melody gasped. "Show some manners, boy. A girl doesn't want to be reminded that she's not looking her best."

Jenna shook her head. "These are my friends?" she said aloud, looking up to the heavens. "No, actually, I'll only have a little scar, where the skin split above the cheekbone. You won't really even notice it, unless you're right up close."

"Oh yeah?" Yoshiko asked. "Does that mean your detective Danny-boy is going to be 'noticing it'?"

"Being right up close and all," Hunter continued.

Jenna raised an eyebrow. "Thanks Hunter. That was for those of us who didn't get Yoshiko's none-too-subtle implication?" She sighed.

"Don't mind my little brother," Melody observed. "The boy's just jealous."

Hunter blushed bright pink, started to stammer something, and stopped when Yoshiko laughed out loud at him. He glared at her. Yoshiko glared back.

"You're cute when you blush," she told him.

Now it was Jenna's turn to stare. Yoshiko had just flirted openly with a boy. If Adam Sandler's movie career weren't proof enough, she figured this was a major sign that Western civilization was crumbling. When Yoshiko looked over at her, Jenna winked.

Keb' Mo' had just gone into a funky rendition of "Just Like You," and Jenna paused to listen a moment—and to eat another forkful of jambalaya—before bothering to respond.

"What about it, Jenna?" Melody asked. "Do you think 'Detective Danny' is going to start romancing you?"

Jenna swallowed. She looked around at her friends thoughtfully. "Nah," she said at last. "I told you guys before, he's too old for me. Sure, he's cute. But it would be just too weird. Besides, why would he want to go out with a college kid?"

"You're not just any college kid, Blake," Yoshiko said admiringly.

Jenna was about to respond when Hunter snorted laughter. "Oh, please, ladies. She's got you both in full-harness gossip mode. Our Miss Jenna isn't speculating about that detective right now because it just wouldn't be polite. Not when she has a date next week."

Jenna smiled demurely as Yoshiko and Melody stared at her. Then she frowned at Hunter.

"How'd you know?" she asked him.

"He told me himself."

"But he just asked tonight," Jenna insisted.

"I saw him right before we left," Hunter explained.

"Him who?" Melody and Yoshiko demanded, simultaneously.

Jenna smiled. "Damon Harris."

"Wait, you hate him," Melody reminded her. "He blew you off because you work with dead folks."

"Yeah, but then she almost got killed, and helped to uncover an international murder conspiracy," Hunter noted.

"But you hate him!" Yoshiko said loudly.

"Hate is such a strong word," Jenna told them, and winced at the pain in her cheek when she smiled.

There was a long pause then, as they all listened to the music. After a while, when they were all done with their meals, and Jenna was sipping a fresh lemonade, she paused and looked around at her friends once more. Her mind was filled with the horrors of the past few weeks, and thoughts about how fortunate she truly was to have made good friends in such a short time.

"Nickel for your thoughts," Melody said, looking at her with concern.

"Nothing much," Jenna shrugged. "It's just . . . the first day of classes, my professor dropped dead. The second day, I assisted at his autopsy. In the first two weeks at college, my father and I each had two attempts made on our lives."

She chuckled. They all stared at her like she was crazy. Then they all began to laugh a little right along with her.

"Yeah," Jenna said, brushing back her long auburn hair. "Let's just hope I don't have to go through four years of this."

about the author

CHRISTOPHER GOLDEN is a novelist, journalist, and comic book writer. His novels include the vampire epics *Of Saints and Shadows; Angel Souls & Devil Hearts*, and *Of Masques and Martyrs*; as well as such media tie-ins as *Buffy the Vampire Slayer: Child of the Hunt* (which he co-wrote with Nancy Holder); *Hellboy: The Lost Army*; and the current hardcover *X-Men: Codename Wolverine*. He is one of the authors of the recently released book *The Watcher's Guide: The Official Companion to Buffy the Vampire Slayer*.

Golden's comic book work includes the Marvel Knights relaunch of *The Punisher*; as well as *Punisher/Wolverine: Revelation, Batman: Real World*; and Wildstorm's *Night Tribes*. His other work includes stints on *The Crow, Spider-Man Unlimited, Buffy the Vampire Slayer*, and the one-shot *Blade: Crescent City Blues*.

Before becoming a full-time writer, he was licensing manager for *Billboard* magazine in New York, where he worked on Fox Television's *Billboard Music Awards* and *American Top 40* radio, among many other projects.

Golden was born and raised in Massachusetts, where he still lives with his family. He graduated from Tufts University. He has recently completed a new, original dark fantasy entitled *Strangewood*, which will be published in 1999 by Penguin Putnam. Please visit him at www.christophergolden.com.

Turn the page for
a preview of
the next
Body of Evidence thriller

THIEF OF HEARTS

Available fall 1999

Murder itself held no pleasure for him. It was what came after—that was what he lived for.

It was just after eight on a Wednesday night. Though the sky was clear, the early October breeze blew cold across Harvard Square. This place, he knew, was the mecca for students all over the area, from Harvard and M.I.T. and Somerset, and others. Even mid-week, what surrounded him now was a sea of college students, wave after wave of dyed hair and piercings and torn and drooping clothing. There were plenty of others, as well, the kids who were less conspicuous. In fact, they were the majority.

But all he saw in the vast sea of flesh were the loud ones, the colorful ones, the ones the others all seemed to gravitate to. He was excited by them, and thrilled that he had found one with charisma, and inner strength, and confidence. They wouldn't all be that way. He wasn't allowed to choose the ones he would have wanted. Nature chose for him.

But this one was something special. He was eager to be close to her. So close. Soon, they would be together.

Kelsey Zarin looked good, and she knew it. But she still enjoyed hearing her friends tell her. She wore beaded denim flairs and a top that was too tight by far, and her hair was a severe mess, with a screaming red strand hanging down in front of her face.

"Hey!"

Kelsey turned at the shout, and saw Caitie Abrams coming up the stairs from the T station, along with a bunch of other people just regurgitated from the subway. With a smile and a flap of her arms, Kelsey started toward her friend.

"Dude!" Kelsey said, rolling her eyes. "You are *so* late. I told those guys to go on, that we'd come find them."

Caitie looked panicked a moment. "You have my ticket, though, right?"

For half a second, Kelsey thought about pretending not to, but Caitie seemed totally wigged, so she just nodded and grabbed the other girl by the arm. Greek Tragedy was playing at Delgado's, and they were lucky enough to have tickets. No way was she going to miss it for Caitie. In fact, if the other girl hadn't shown up in another two minutes, Kelsey would have just bagged on her and given the ticket to some poor lost soul on the street.

Or sold it for fun and profit.

They walked out of the center of the square, down toward the Charles River. The Square had always been trendy, but Kelsey was kind of bummed that she hadn't been here before it had gotten so commercial. People talked all the time about what it had been like before Gap was on, like, every corner. Still, it was cool. There were plenty of non-chain businesses, and that was always a good thing. There were about a million specialty and used book shops in Harvard Square, not to mention the best ice cream on God's green earth, and some spicy restaurants.

College was all right, as far as Kelsey was concerned. But without Harvard Square, it would be too boring for words. She was brilliant. She had known that before M.I.T. had offered her a free ride, all four years. But she just didn't like to study. Being able to hang in the Square and party with her friends all the time—that was a decent trade-off for laying the groundwork for a future in physics at NASA, or whatever.

They passed The Garage, and the travel agent where they had that sign that said "Please Go Away," which she'd always liked, and then they were crossing Mt. Auburn Street.

"I am so psyched for this show," Caitie squealed. "I can't believe I missed that BNL concert last week, but this'll make up for it."

Kelsey raised her eyebrows. She didn't say anything, but she thought, *Just keep telling yourself that. As if.*

Then they were at Delgado's. There wasn't a line. Anyone with tickets was already inside, and anyone else was just screwed. Once upon a time, way back in the eighteen hundreds, Delgado's had been a huge tavern in Harvard Square. Then, for a few decades, it had become a little, offbeat marketplace for weird jewelry and clothes. Then, sometime in the eighties, it became Delgado's.

It had somehow managed to remain cool ever since. If a band was cutting edge enough, but not popular enough to fill the Orpheum, they played Delgado's. The music was always good, but Greek Tragedy was an act on their way up, so tonight was something really special.

As they passed their tickets to the bouncer at the door, Kelsey put her hand on Caitie's arm.

"What's up?" Caitie asked as they went through the door into the dull roar of conversation that had built up in anticipation of the band's starting.

"You and me," Kelsey said. "We're cool about Ryan, right? I mean, you don't mind if I . . ."

Caitie smiled bitterly, and then shrugged. "He didn't want me, Kels. Maybe you'll have more luck."

Kelsey rolled her eyes. "You make it sound so cheap and tawdry."

"There's a reason for that," Caitie said, and her smile made it clear she wasn't really joking.

Kelsey didn't care.

She thought she and Ryan made a good pair. It was obvious he liked her. As long as she'd covered her ass with Caitie, she figured it was worth a shot. He was a good guy, and she wanted to spend more time with him.

They shoved their way through the crowd at the bar until the room opened up to make space for a bunch of round tables surrounded by chairs. Beyond that was a cleared space for people who couldn't sit still and had to butcher the concept of dancing. Beyond that was the stage. An old-time curtain was hung across it, and Kelsey could hear the distant clash of a cymbal and the rumbling thunder of someone testing out the drum kit.

She hadn't been all that psyched about seeing Greek Tragedy. They were really good, but not as good as her friends seemed to think. But now she was changing her mind. Delgado's was a very cool place to be. And she'd be with Ryan.

"There they are," Caitie said, and tugged on her hand.

The other girl shouldered through the gathering crowd and Kelsey followed right behind her. A well-placed elbow got her through a couple of tight spots. Then she looked up and saw Ryan and Nicky and Barb and Ashley. They'd saved a pair of seats for Caitie and Kelsey, but Kelsey barely noticed.

All she saw was how close Ryan and Ashley were sitting. And the little grin on Ash's face that said it all.

"Damn it," she cursed under her breath.

Then she just sighed. "Story of my life."

"What?" Caitie called, over the murmur of the crowd.

"Nothing," Kelsey said, and shook her head.

No sooner had they greeted everyone and taken their seats than the lights dimmed and the curtain was drawn and the five maniacs who made up Greek Tragedy thrashed into a party song that had Kelsey smiling and bopping along in no time.

To hell with Ryan, she thought, about halfway through the third song. *I can do better.*

As the fifth song began, Kelsey got up to go to the bathroom. She shouldered her way through gyrating college kids until she reached the bar, which was even tighter. Finally, she made it to the long hallway where the two bathrooms were.

The lines were brutal. There were at least a dozen girls waiting.

"Oh, great," she muttered. "I'm not meeting Mr. Right if I pee my pants."

"Probably true," said a male voice.

Kelsey turned, eyes wide, and looked up into the face of a guy she'd never seen before. Her cheeks flushed red with embarrassment, and she looked away, trying not to laugh.

"Sorry," the guy said, also doing his polite best not to laugh. "Couldn't help overhearing. Y'know, if you need to go that bad, there's another john. It's supposed to be just for employees, but people always end up using it at these shows."

Now she perked up. She really did have to go. "Really? Where is it?"

The guy smiled kindly. "End of the hall, before the door to the kitchen, there's one marked 'emergency exit only.' Through that, down the bottom of the stairs."

Still slightly embarrassed, Kelsey tossed her thick strand of wild red hair away from her face and grinned sheepishly.

"Thanks," she said. "When I get back, I'll buy you a beer."

"I'll take you up on that," the guy said.

Kelsey followed her savior's directions, pushed through the door, hoping that no alarms would go off, and then started down the stairs. The noise from the bar was really loud, even down here. The sound of feet stamping on old floorboards filled the stairwell. It wasn't very well lit, but she started down, her bladder commanding her to continue.

At the bottom of the stairs, she looked around, mystified. She saw only a metal door which obviously led outside, and a small wooden door set into a crooked frame. The building really was ancient. In the half-light, she moved over to the small door, thinking there might be rats or something, and if that was the case, well, her bladder would just have to wait.

At the little door, she grabbed the knob and gave it a twist. It stuck at first, but she put a little weight behind it and it squeaked open. It was dark inside, and Kelsey reached in and felt around for a light switch. She found it, and flicked the light on. It flickered to life, and for a moment, she just stared.

It was a storage closet. Mop, bucket, that sort of thing. And it was the only room down here.

"Oh, man," she said angrily. "What a jerk."

Then she let out a small yelp as a powerful hand clamped over her mouth, and she was yanked violently against the chest of the man standing behind her.

"Now is that nice?" the man asked amiably, as he drew the scalpel across her throat, severing her carotid artery and her larynx.

He held her so the spurting blood would not spray him, and she struggled and tried to scream. With her larynx cut, she could make only the most pitiful sounds. Surely nothing that would be heard upstairs. Eventually, she fell limp against him, and he laid her down. With the scalpel, he cut away her clothes.

He told himself there was nothing improper in that act. He was only doing it, after all, to expose her chest. Quickly, he removed his tools from the pockets inside his coat.

Then he set about his work.

It was no simple task, removing a human heart. But he'd grown quite adept at it over the past few months.

Look for the next
Body of Evidence **thriller**
THIEF OF HEARTS
by
Christopher Golden
Available from Pocket Books
Fall 1999

BODY OF EVIDENCE THRILLERS
Starring Jenna Blake

"The first day at college, my professor dropped dead. The second day, I assisted at his autopsy. Let's hope I don't have to go through four years of this...."

When Jenna Blake starts her freshman year at Somerset University, it's an exciting time, filled with new faces and new challenges, not to mention parties and guys and...a job interview with the medical examiner that takes place in the middle of an autopsy! As Jenna starts her new job, she is drawn into a web of dangerous politics and deadly disease...a web that will bring her face to face with a pair of killers: one medical, and one all too human.

Body Bags
(Available May 1999)

Thief of Hearts
(Available August 1999)

Soul Survivor
(Available November 1999)

BY CHRISTOPHER GOLDEN
Bestselling coauthor of
Buffy the Vampire Slayer™ The Watcher's Guide

Published by Pocket Books

In time of tragedy,
a love that would not die...

Hindenburg, 1937
By Cameron Dokey

San Francisco Earthquake, 1906
By Kathleen Duey

Chicago Fire, 1871
By Elizabeth Massie

Washington Avalanche, 1910
By Cameron Dokey

---

sweeping stories of star-crossed romance

Starting in July 1999

From Archway Paperbacks
Published by Pocket Books